VIKING
ATTACK

LEGACY PRESS

LegacyPressKids.com

VIKING ATTACK

A
TIME CRASHERS
Adventure

BY

H. MICHAEL BREWER

DEDICATION: For Mark, Amy, Colman, and the housefly

TIME CRASHERS: VIKING ATTACK
©2014 by Michael Brewer, third printing
ISBN 10: 1-58411-135-6
ISBN 13: 978-1-58411-135-1
Legacy reorder# LP48701
JUVENILE FICTION / Religious / Christian / General

Legacy Press
P.O. Box 261129
San Diego, CA 92196
www.LegacyPressKids.com

Cover illustrator: Dave Carleson
Interior illustrators: Aburtov and Graphikslava

Unless otherwise noted, Scriptures are from the *Holy Bible: New International* Version (North American Edition), ©1973, 1978, 1984 by the International Bible Society. Used by permission of Zondervan Bible Publishers.

Printed in the United States of America

TABLE OF CONTENTS

INTRODUCTION 6

FRIENDS 8

VIKING VENTURES ...29, 39, 43, 50, 89, 91, 112, 140, 156, 177, 183

EPILOGUE 194

THE REAL DEAL 197

Introduction

E than Conway's father, a brilliant scientist, has been experimenting with time travel. Now Dr. Conway is missing and Ethan fears his father is lost somewhere in the past. Ethan has studied his father's files and learned how to operate the time machine.

According to Dr. Conway's notes, the machine is programmed for thirty-three different trips into history. Those were trial runs, launching objects or animals into the past and safely retrieving them. Finally, the scientist used the machine to send himself on a time trip. At least that's what Ethan believes.

Did something go wrong? Is Dr. Conway trapped in the past? Has he been injured? Does he need help? Ethan is certain of only one thing. His father would never willingly leave him. If his father hasn't returned, it's because he can't. So Ethan will become a time traveler. He'll find his dad and bring him home.

Ethan won't make the trip alone. His two best friends will join him in the adventure: Jake Bradley, a natural athlete, and Spencer Price, a young genius and walking database.

And *you* will take part in the adventure, too. You'll journey into the past with Ethan, Jake, and Spencer. You'll face the same dangers and you'll help them make life-or-death decisions. How this story turns out is up to you!

The machine will send the Time Crashers on one of the thirty-three programmed trips into the past. There's no way to know what lies ahead. You don't know where you'll go or which trip might lead to Ethan's lost father. Maybe you'll come face to face with pirates or Wild West outlaws or dinosaurs. Once you are thrown into the past, your own actions will decide whether you succeed or fail. You need bravery, quick wits, and lots of prayer to face the dangers of a long-ago world. Each choice opens a different path and confronts you with even more decisions. Choose carefully. The fate of the Time Crashers is in *your* hands.

WHEN YOU ARE READY
TO BEGIN THE ADVENTURE,
TURN THE PAGE. ⟹

Friends

Ethan Conway stands in the dim light of his father's lab, hidden in a secret room beneath the basement of their home. The dank air smells of damp concrete and the bittersweet tang of the power crystal as it energizes the time machine.

Ethan's two best friends are in the lab, too. On his right is Jake Bradley, captain of the school football team. In fact, he plays every sport in school. With wide shoulders and buzz-cut blond hair, Jake looks a like a young movie hero. His blue eyes watch Ethan with an easy-going expression. In a tight spot, Ethan knows he can count on Jake to guard his back.

On Ethan's other side is Spencer Price. In some ways he is Jake's opposite. He is a head shorter than the football player and prefers reading books to running bases. He is captain of the Academic Team and aces every test in every subject. Maybe there's a topic Spencer doesn't know about, but Ethan and Jake haven't found it.

"So this is the time machine?" Spencer asks, his curious gaze darting around the room, studying the LED indicator and controls. He leans close to the power crystal and ruby light falls across his dark face.

Ethan nods. "Awesome, isn't it?"

Standing side by side, the three friends watch the blinking lights on the machine: Ethan on one side, Spencer, the shortest, on the other, and Jake, the tallest, in the middle. Ethan smiles, wondering how people who are so different can be such close friends. He says to his pals, "I'm not sure you should come on this  trip. We're going into the unknown. I couldn't stand it if you got hurt helping me find Dad."

Spencer rolls his eyes.

"Like I'll pass up a chance to visit the past," he says. "We might

meet William Shakespeare or visit the ancient library of Alexandria." Jake makes snoring sounds.

"Or do something not totally boring, like watching the first Olympics," says Jake, punching Ethan's shoulder. "Anyway, you wouldn't last five minutes without us. If a wooly mammoth squashes you into an Ethan pancake, we have to find a new Musketeer to take your place."

"If we make enough trips into the past, Jake might actually score a B on one of Mr. Nutt's history exams," Spencer teases.

Ethan ignores the good-natured joking. Should he put his friends at risk? Can these three face the dangers of time travel? Making the trip alone is scary, but is it right to drag Jake and Spencer along?

"What are the chances of finding my father?" Ethan asks. "This whole idea might be foolish. Maybe I should turn off the time machine, seal up the secret lab, and get on with my life. I miss Dad, but isn't it better to have one person lost in time than to lose three more?"

What should Ethan do?

 IF YOU THINK ETHAN SHOULD CANCEL THE TIME TRIP, TURN TO **PAGE 12.**

 IF YOU THINK ETHAN AND HIS FRIENDS SHOULD USE THE TIME MACHINE, TURN TO **PAGE 14.**

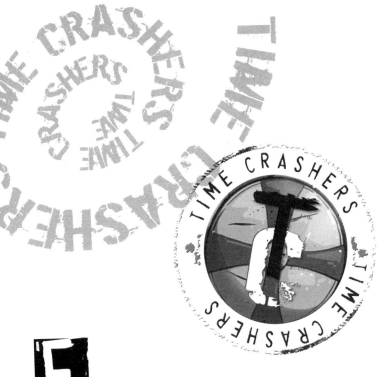

Ethan's shoulders slump as he studies the time machine.

"It wouldn't be right," he tells his friends. "I see that now. How can I risk our lives on this crazy plan? We might end up in the middle of a pre-historic ocean, treading water until some dinosaur gobbles us up."

"Munched by a mosasaur," Spencer says. "Or dinner for a dakosaurus."

Both buddies look disappointed, but it's Jake who asks, "Are you sure? We're with you all the way."

Ethan shakes his head again. With a sigh, he flips a toggle and the humming machine powers down, growing silent. The power crystal dims to a faint glow. Nobody speaks as Ethan leads them up the stairs from the sub-basement lab. He locks the door behind them.

TIME CRASHERS

Years later, Ethan decides he made a mistake in giving up on his father. He returns to the hidden room and tries to activate the time machine. But the controls won't energize. The power crystal has died. The time machine will never work again.

Sad and regretful, Ethan Conway leaves the lab for good. He never sees his father again.

THE END

YOU DON'T LIKE THIS ENDING?

DO YOU WISH ETHAN HAD MADE OTHER CHOICES?
GOOD NEWS! YOU TOO HAVE A TIME MACHINE.
GO BACK AND DO IT DIFFERENTLY.

THE FINAL ENDING IS UP TO YOU.

et's do it," Ethan says to his friends. "Everything has risk. A football game, a bicycle ride, a science fair project."

"Especially Spencer's science experiments," Jake says with a grin.

"One little explosion," Spencer groans, "and I can't live it down. At least I don't dress like I'm on safari."

He waves a hand at Jake's outfit: a pair of cargo pants and a photographer's vest.

"Exactly how many pockets do you have?" Ethan asks.

Jake reddens and he mumbles, "Fifty-seven."

"Carrying what?" Spencer asks.

"Stuff we might need," Jake says defensively. "A Swiss army knife, fishing line, water-proof matches, a laser pointer…"

Spencer explodes with laughter. "If we need a laser pointer on this trip, I'll eat that jacket, zippers and all."

"It's like Batman's utility belt, only better. You'll see!" Jake slams his fist into his palm. "The Three Amigos are on their way to make history."

"Four if you count God," Spencer says, "and I'm really counting on the Big Guy in the sky."

The U-shaped time machine fills most of the room. From floor to ceiling it covers three walls. The trio stands inside the hollow of the horseshoe shape. Ethan presses a green button on the control panel. The button begins to blink.

"Ten seconds!" Ethan shouts over the hum of the machine.

The boys hurry onto a metal plate installed in the floor, the time machine wrapped around them. Ethan shivers as an eerie vibration tingles up and down his spine. His skin prickles as if tickled by needles. On the back of his neck, tiny hairs stand up like soldiers springing to attention. The power crystal bathes the lab in blood-red light. Ethan gulps as his stomach flops. The shrill hum fills the basement, growing louder and louder. And louder!

Just when Ethan fears the wailing will mush his brain into oatmeal, the clamor abruptly stops. The lab vanishes. Wisps of gray fog replace the red glow. Instead of polished metal, Ethan stands on dewy clover. The perfume of wild flowers floats in the air. Waves lap nearby.

"Are we there yet?" Jake whispers.

Something looms in the fog. A pre-historic beast? A giant warrior? Ethan's gaze pierces the mist. A cross carved from solid rock rises above the boys. Strange, twisting animals and stunted human shapes are engraved on the twelve-foot slab, all figures brightly painted. In the center of the cross, where the arms meet the shaft, is a stone circle. Within the circle, a carved Jesus hangs with hands spread wide.

"It's a high cross," Spencer exclaims. "Irish monks created these a thousand years ago."

"A thousand years?" Ethan asks in wonder.

Spencer nods. A huge smile spreads across his face.

"We're in ancient Ireland," Spencer says. "Or maybe Scotland."

"Guess again," says a scornful voice.

Ethan spins around and spots a pretty girl in a ragged dress with a basket of woven grass under her arm. A floppy wool hat perches on her short-cropped hair. She eyes the boys defiantly. A black and brown dog peers between her legs, growling faintly.

"Northumbria," she mocks. "That's where you are."

"The east coast of northern England," Spencer explains, turning to the girl. "What is the year?"

The girl shakes her head, her brown eyes skeptical. "The Year of our Lord 793. Everyone knows that."

Jake glances at Ethan and says, "I guess the language doohickey works."

Ethan nods, grateful that his father built a translation app into the time travel device. Wherever and whenever the boys travel, the translation app will allow them to talk to local people in their own language. Even though the Time Crashers have landed in England, twelve-hundred year old English is a totally different language. Ethan introduces himself and his friends to the girl.

"I'm Rachel," she tells them.

"We are strangers," Ethan admits.

"Stranger than anyone I know," Rachel says. Her eyes turn toward Spencer. "I've never seen anyone with such dark skin."

"You'll never meet another Spencer," Jake quips.

"Can you help us find our way?" Ethan inquires.

Rachel gestures toward the sea sounds. "The monastery is that way, a muddy walk, but easy."

Spencer's voice trembles. "The Monastery of Lindisfarne?"

"Of course." Rachel rolls her eyes. "Holy Isle."

Ethan and Jake trade smiles. Spencer is so revved up he seems to vibrate. But this is a rescue mission, not a field trip. When Spencer opens his mouth to ask more questions, Ethan interrupts.

"We're looking for a traveler," Ethan says to the girl. "A tall man with red hair like mine." He touches his cheek. "Right here he has a

birthmark shaped like a half moon."

Rachel shrugs.

"My sister Bethany might know such a man." She jerks a thumb over her shoulder. "We live in the woods."

Now she points again into the distance behind the boys. "Or you could ask the monks on Holy Isle."

"I need to talk with my friends," Ethan tells Rachel. The three boys move away from the ragged girl.

"What do you think?" Ethan asks in a low voice.

"Rachel knows her way around," says Jake. "We should stick with her."

"Holy Isle was a bright light in a dark world," Spencer argues. "Do you want to pass up the chance to see a center of learning that changed history?"

"Whatever we decide, we have to return here within thirty hours," Ethan reminds his friends. "Once each hour, the time machine will send a retrieval pulse to this spot. If we're here, the pulse will bring us home. If we miss it, we have to wait for the next pulse."

"What happens after thirty hours?" Jake asks.

"The time machine shuts down," Ethan explains. "We'll be trapped."

"Goodbye cell phones and rocky road ice cream," Jake groans. "Get me to the removal bus on time."

"Retrieval pulse," Spencer corrects his friend.

"It won't matter what we call it," says Jake, "if we miss it."

As his friends joke, Ethan wonders whether to follow the girl or go to the monastery. When facing a hard decision, sometimes Ethan turns to the Bible for help. Reaching into the pocket of his jeans, he pulls out a small electronic tablet. The mini-reader contains the text of the whole Bible. Ethan jabs the screen and the tablet displays a random verse from the Bible. It's like opening a Bible to no page in particular and reading the first words the eye falls on. Sometimes the verse helps, sometimes it doesn't. Why not try it?

But the screen jumbles the verse. Traveling through time must have damaged the tablet. Ethan can't make sense of the words.

What will Ethan do next?

 IF YOU THINK HE SHOULD FOLLOW RACHEL, TURN TO **PAGE 22**.

 IF YOU THINK HE SHOULD GO TO HOLY ISLE, TURN TO **PAGE 69**.

Although he can't read the verse, Ethan remembers the Bible taught him to have faith. As long as he keeps looking, there is hope of finding his father. Ethan decides to accompany Rachel. If he learns nothing from her sister, the boys can visit the monastery next.

With the dog leading the way, Rachel guides the three friends along a narrow path winding among old trees.

"What's in the basket?" Ethan asks.

"Shellfish," Rachel says. "I come to the shore every day to gather cockles and mussels."

"Have you seen other strangers on the shore?" Ethan asks. "Someone like us near the stone cross?"

She glances away. "No, I've never seen anyone…like you…

near the cross."

The path leads into a daisy-speckled clearing. On the far side of the meadow squats a small house of sticks and mud. Thick grass grows on the mud roof. A girl wearing a patched wool dress and sandals sits on a stool in front of the doorway. She resembles Rachel, with longer, lighter hair.

She looks up from the flop-eared rabbit resting in her lap and surveys the visitors with curious eyes.

"Bethany," Rachel calls, "I've brought guests. I found them at the cross."

Ethan wonders about the glance that passes between the sisters.

"They are looking for a man with red hair and a half moon on his cheek," Rachel continues.

Bethany nods thoughtfully.

"He doesn't enjoy visitors," the older sister says, "but from the look of your clothes, you've come a long way. I suppose there's no harm in showing you where he lives."

A weight lifts from Ethan's heart. "The man I described is here?"

"A little further along the path," Bethany says. "We can take you there." She smoothes the rabbit's fur and sets it on the grass.

Rachel addresses her dog, "Draca, stay here and keep the rabbit company. I'll be back soon." The dog's ears and tail fall, and his head slumps. Looking disappointed, Draca curls up in a sunny spot.

"Is it far?" Ethan blurts. "Is he healthy? He lives alone? When did he come here?"

"So many questions," Bethany snorts. "Ask him yourself."

Birds chirp overhead, taking wing as the walkers wind along the path. With a flash of red, a fox slinks into the bushes. Nearby, a hungry woodpecker hammers a tree.

"Be careful of the sinkhole," Rachel calls over her shoulder.

"How big?" Spencer asks. "Can we take a look?"

Bethany shrugs. "Over this way."

They leave the path and push through a tangle of blackberry bushes. Pinching a thorny branch carefully between two fingers, Bethany lifts it. "Through there," she says, holding the briars back. The boys duck under the thorns and gawk at a hole big enough to swallow a school bus. The sides of the sinkhole fall away, the bottom larger than the top.

"Wow," Spencer breathes in amazement. "That is quite a—"

Suddenly Spencer topples forward, pushed by Rachel. At the same instant, Ethan feels a determined hand on his own back. He and Jake fly over the edge, arms wind-milling. They sploosh into soft mud at the bottom of the hole.

"Why did you do that?" Jake yells, wiping mud from his face. "We haven't done anything to you! Take us to the man!"

"There is no man," Bethany calls. "I just pretended."

"They are witches," Rachel says solemnly. "They appeared by the cross out of nothing, just like before."

"I told you we should have killed the other one," Bethany says, wagging a finger at her younger sister. "Now we have three more on our doorstep. What's next? A whole army of the devil?"

"The first one seemed harmless," Rachel tells her sister, "but not

these. That one carries a devil stone that makes strange letters."

Ethan groans. She must have seen his tablet. Of course, it looks like magic to her.

"You've made a mistake," Ethan calls to the girls. "Don't leave us here."

"You'll stay there until one of the monks looks you over," Bethany declares. Glaring at her sister, she adds, "We should have summoned the Abbot when the other one came."

"How were we to know?" Rachel protests. "He seemed sweet."

"Bring the monk," Ethan begs. "We'll explain everything."

Bethany shrugs.

"The monk comes once a week to buy herbs and tea from us," Bethany says. "He'll be along in two or three days."

The friends exchange worried glances. In thirty hours the time machine shuts down and they will be trapped in this era. If they can't get out of this sinkhole…

"Please, listen to me," Ethan calls.

Bethany puts fingers in her ears and shouts, "We won't hear your tempting talk. The devil is the father of lies."

She disappears from the edge of the hole. After staring down a moment longer, Rachel also backs out of view.

"Let's get climbing," Jake suggests.

But climbing is impossible. The soft dirt crumbles and slides beneath their feet and clawing hands. Worse yet, the earthen walls curve inward toward the top, creating a slope only a fly could cross. Soon the boys are breathless, mud-encrusted, and discouraged.

"We could dig," Spencer suggests. "Sinkholes indicate cave country. We might discover an underground passage."

"Or we could sing hymns," Ethan says.

"Sing hymns?" Jake asks.

"Sure," Ethan says. "That's what Paul and Silas did when they were in prison. They sang songs to God, and God got them out of jail."

IF YOU THINK THE BOYS SHOULD TRY TO DIG OUT OF THE SINKHOLE, TURN TO **PAGE 30**.

IF YOU THINK THEY SHOULD SING HYMNS, TURN TO **PAGE 41**.

TALK LIKE A VIKING

The Time Crashers have a language app to help them understand the natives and Vikings of this ancient land. You might be surprised that you already know some Viking words that long ago entered the English language. The next time you use these words, remember that we learned them from the Vikings.

To figure out the words, add the missing vowels (A, E, I, O, U, or Y).

_____ NG _____ R

BL _____ _____ M

KN _____ F _____

CR _____ WL

W _____ NG

H _____ SB _____ ND

SK _____ LL

SK _____

TR _____ ST

SC _____ R _____

SK _____ RT

W _____ ND _____ W

_____ GL _____

WR _____ NG

K _____ D

L _____ FT

DI _____

F _____ LL _____ W

ANSWERS: anger, bloom, knife, crawl, wing, husband, skill, sky, trust, scare, skirt, window, ugly, wrong, kid, lift, die, fellow

’m for digging," Jake says. "If that doesn't get us anywhere, then we can sing."

"A man of action," Ethan declares. "Okay, I can use the exercise."

The boys root around in the sinkhole. Jake locates a pointed stone the size of a pizza slice. Ethan and Spencer each find broken limbs.

"Where do we start?" Jake asks.

"Water's trickling from this side," Spencer points out. "That's our best bet."

The moist mud carves away easily, sliding loose in small avalanches. Soon they dig a closet-sized hole in the pit wall. Jake takes point, gouging at the earth, while Spencer and Ethan pull loose mud out of the way.

"Hey," Jake shouts. "I think we're getting somewhere."

The other two crowd forward to peer at a dark hole in the mud wall. Together they dig frantically, and the hole enlarges. A slab of mud collapses, opening into an underground passage.

"Amazing!" Spencer bursts out. "Who thought this would work?"

They push through the opening and immediately a light clicks on.

"Miniature flashlight," Jake crows to Spencer, "from my utility vest. Now who's laughing?"

"Not me, big guy," Spencer says.

They duck walk through the muddy passage until it opens into a limestone cave where they stand upright. In the flashlight's glow they skirt pools of dark water and duck overhanging rocks. Soon the cave forks.

"I've got the bright light," Jake says. "Anybody got a bright idea?"

"Do you have matches?" Spencer asks.

Jake draws out a small box. "Waterproof matches," Jake informs his pal.

"That will be handy if we need to burn any water," Spencer says. He strikes a match. The flame flares, burns for a moment, then dies.

"Point the light this way," Spencer says. Smoke trickles from the dead match and drifts toward the right hand tunnel. Spencer nods in the direction of the smoke. "Air flow. This tunnel leads outside."

"You are smarter than a barrel of laptops," Jake says with approval.

They creep through the cool cave. For a long time, the only sound is their breathing and wet footsteps. A faint squeal sounds ahead.

"We're close to something," Ethan says. "Do you smell that?"

"Oh, my sinuses," Spencer complains. "That's worse than Jake's gym bag."

The cave veers left. Light appears ahead, a gray glow, then a patch of sky. Jake switches off his flashlight and nearly steps on a squirming knot of pink bodies. He stoops to stare at eight tiny piglets playing king of the hill, snouts snuffling and open mouths squeaking for food.

"These guys are cute," Jake says, reaching forward.

"Don't touch them!" Spencer snaps. "Where there's babies, there's a mama, and we don't want to meet her."

A snarling oink fills the air, and a bloated shape blocks the cave exit.

"Why am I always right?" Spencer grouses.

"It's only a pig, right?" Jake asks.

"No, it's only a wild boar," Spencer corrects him. "This is not a ham sandwich, old buddy. This is dagger-sharp teeth and 200 pounds of motherly bad attitude."

"Got any anti-boar weapons in your utility vest?" Ethan asks. "Bacon slicer? Barbecue grill? Sausage grinder?"

"I've got something," Jake admits, "but I need porky to get closer."

The boar snorts, lowers her head, and charges.

"Be careful!" Spencer shouts. "She'll rip you with those hooves!"

"She's close enough," Ethan yelps.

"Not yet," Jake replies. He tugs a small canister from a zipper pocket.

"Is that crazy string?" Spencer howls. "You can't fight a raging boar with crazy string! We're hoggy chow."

The boar charges, dark eyes glinting. Jake smells its rotten breath. Slobber dribbles from her open mouth.

"Keep coming," Jake coaxes. "A little closer. Got to make this count."

He holds the canister at arm's length, nozzle pointed at the boar.

"Now?" Ethan asks.

"Now!" Jake shouts.

The pepper spray squirts from the can in a steady stream, the thin liquid splashing the pig's

eyes and snout. The boar shrieks and spins in circles, snapping at the air, seeking a target. Snorting and whining, the mother collapses, pawing at her nose and eyes with muddy hooves.

With a pitying glance, Jake leaps over the writhing animal. Ethan and Spencer follow, taking careful steps around the snorting boar. Spencer fans at his eyes, tears tracking down his cheeks.

"That stuff is potent," Spencer says, drying his eyes on his sleeve. Jake coughs and spits.

"Hot pepper juice," Jake says. "Letter carriers use it on mean dogs. It doesn't do any damage, but it sure hurts."

"So Petunia Pig's all right?" Ethan asks.

"Yeah, but she's going to be in a bad mood," Jake says.

"Do we have to walk to the shore?" Spencer asks. "Or do you have a fold-up helicopter in your jacket?"

"No, but I have a fold up genius-basher," Jake says. He holds up one hand and slowly folds the fingers into a fist. "Wanna see how it works?"

"Violence is the first resort of those who lack imagination," Spencer says, making tsk-tsk sounds.

They get their bearings from the sun and head toward the shore. They find the beach in a short while, but not the standing cross, so they trace the waterline north. As they round a spit of land, the cross appears a few yards away.

"Awesome!" Spencer shouts, but the cheer dies on his lips.

A Viking sits cross-legged on the beach, chewing a stick of jerky. He wears baggy wool pants and chain mail over a leather vest. Gobbling the last of the meat, the Viking stands and shakes black hair out of startling blue eyes. In his thin, weathered face, a hawk-beak nose overhangs a black moustache. A sword dangles from his belt. Grinning as he chews, the raider plucks a spear planted in the damp soil. He beckons the friends closer.

"Who is that?" Spencer asks. "The welcoming committee?"

"Maybe a guard," Ethan says. "Maybe a scout."

"Maybe trouble," Jake adds.

"Or all of the above," Spencer says, turning to Jake. "How are you stocked on pepper spray?"

"Empty," Jake says.

Ethan asks, "Anybody got a plan?"

Spencer nods. "Run."

The boys race back along the path toward the cave, pursued by angry curses and thudding footfalls.

"Pour it on," Spencer shouts. "We'll make this guy sorry he got off the boat."

They return to the cave entrance, stomping clear footprints in the mud. Then they step out backwards and leap away, trying not to leave more tracks.

Huddled behind a tumble of boulders, Spencer peeks through a gap. The Viking slows as he approaches the cave. His hatchet face turns toward the ground and he studies the footprints. Satisfied, the Viking stalks into the cave, spear in hand. For a moment silence hangs in the air. Suddenly a chorus of bellowing, snorting, and oinking erupts. The Viking staggers from the cave, stumbles, and drops his spear. Before he can retrieve it, the furious boar charges.

The Viking flees with the angry porker snapping at his backside. The raider leaps and clutches a low-hanging tree branch. He hauls his feet up and dangles from the limb, scrambling to get on top. As he wrestles his weight onto the limb, the sword slips from his belt. The iron blade thumps the ground near the boar. The hog leaps and almost snags a mouthful of Viking.

"That hog has anger issues," Spencer says. "She's going to sit under that tree for a long time, hoping for a Norwegian nosh."

"Too bad the Viking doesn't have a bow and arrow," Ethan says.

"Yeah, a real shame," Jake says. "Should we help him?"

"Let me ask the magic eight-ball," Spencer says. He stares into his empty hand and pretends to read. "Get moving, you three, while the Viking's in the tree."

"The magic eight-ball never lies," Jake says.

They cut across the land, taking a shorter route back to the standing cross. As they walk, Ethan says, "I wonder who was the

other stranger Rachel found on the beach? Remember Bethany said they should have killed him?"

"Are you thinking it might be your dad?" Spencer asks.

Ethan shrugs. "My gut says Dad's not here. That's not scientific, but my gut is usually right."

"Spider-sense," Jake nods. "You gotta pay attention."

"Maybe we should check the island to be sure," Spencer says.

 TURN TO **PAGE 40**.

THE MYSTERIOUS VISITOR

Would you like to find out the identity of the mysterious "other stranger" Rachel found on the beach near the cross? Look up the name of the land where Noah's ark landed on a mountaintop. You can find that in Genesis 8:4. Fill in the last four letters of the country's name in the blanks below.

If you'd like, you can draw the visitor into the picture.

WHEN DR. CONWAY WAS TESTING THE TIME MACHINE, HE SENT

———

— — — —

INTO THE PAST.

Answer: A RAT

I f we don't visit Lindisfarne, I'll always wonder if Dad was there and we missed him,"

Ethan decides. "We haven't been here long. We can still visit Holy Isle and get back in plenty of time to catch the retrieval pulse."

"Yeah," Jake shouts. He slaps a high-five with Spencer.

They emerge from the trees and head toward the beach. Jake holds up a warning hand. He points toward the stone cross. A dark-robed figure sits at the foot of the cross, leaning against the shaft. As they tiptoe closer, the boys see that his chin rests on his chest and his eyes are closed.

"Whoa!" Spencer says. "Who is this guy?"

 TURN TO **PAGE 68**.

Hymns are prayers set to music," Spencer agrees, "and prayer is always a good idea." He sings a praise chorus about Jesus being Lord and King. Jake and Ethan know the song from Sunday school, and they join in. They sing song after song, hymns about God's love and power.

"I feel better," Jake says.

"That's because we're focusing on God instead of our problems," Ethan tells him.

"Here's a song about God *and* our problems," Spencer says. "I know you've never heard it because I just made it up."

Jake and Ethan clap and cheer as Spencer sings:

Trusting Jesus is my goal, even when I'm in a hole.

He will bring us safely through, He loves me and He loves you.

Come get me, Jesus! Come get me, Jesus!

Come get me, Jesus! Please get me out of here!

Jesus never lets us down, even ten yards underground.

Though the mud is to my knees, Jesus hears and Jesus sees.

Come get me, Jesus! Come get me, Jesus!

Come get me, Jesus! Please get me out of here!

TURN TO PAGE 44.

SAY IT WITH MUSIC

Have you ever written a song? It's not that hard!

First, pick an easy tune, something like *Jesus Loves Me* or *Row, Row, Row Your Boat*.

Second, decide what you want to sing about. Maybe your song will be about the wonderful things God created in this beautiful world: "God made sun and stars and trees, God made sharks and bumblebees…"

Once you have a tune and a subject, you can go to work. Find words that will make your idea fit your tune.

Write your song on this page.

Spencer ends his song to the applause of his friends. From overhead, a girl's voice calls out, "You're singing about Jesus!"

Rachel peers over the sinkhole's lip. Draca the dog looks down, too.

"Witches wouldn't sing about the holy Lord Jesus," Rachel declares, puzzled.

"That proves we aren't witches," Ethan says. "We are followers of Jesus."

Rachel's mouth turns into a round O and her eyebrows leap up. Her face disappears and a short while later a twisty length of grapevine snakes over the edge.

"I wrapped it around a tree," Rachel calls.

"Start with the smallest," Jake says. He hands the vine to Spencer who clambers to the top. Ethan follows, then Jake.

"Thank you, Rachel," Ethan says.

"We should never have thrown you down there," a teary Rachel confesses. "We thought you were the devil's servants."

"You don't have to be afraid of us, but I have a question," Ethan tells the girl. "You mentioned someone else appearing at the cross by magic. Was it the man I described?"

"It wasn't a man," she admits. "It was a rat in a cage."

"Black? With one white paw and a white tip on its tail?" Ethan asks.

Rachel nods, her eyes wide.

"One of Dad's lab rats." Ethan tells his friends, "The one we called Frostbite."

"Dr. Conway must have sent Frostbite to see if living things could move through time," Spencer guesses.

"And Rachel carried the cage away before the retrieval pulse could bring the rat home," Jake says.

"Did I do wrong?" Rachel quavers.

"No," Ethan reassures her. "What happened to the rat?"

"We thought it might be from the devil," Rachel says, "but it seemed a harmless thing. I turned it loose in the woods."

"I'm glad Frostbite is okay," Ethan says, smiling.

"Will you come back to our house for herb tea?" Rachel asks. "I feel badly about how we've treated you."

IF YOU THINK THE BOYS SHOULD RETURN TO RACHEL'S HOUSE, SEE THE **NEXT PAGE**.

IF YOU THINK THE BOYS SHOULD HEAD BACK TO THE BEACH, TURN TO **PAGE 58**.

than glances at his companions. Jake and Spencer shrug.

"Will your sister Bethany mind?" Ethan asks Rachel.

"Not when I tell her you are followers of Jesus," she says.

Once again Draca takes the lead on the meandering trail. Occasionally he glares at the boys, growling in his throat.

"Your dog doesn't like us," Jake says.

"Draca doesn't like anybody but me," Rachel says, smiling merrily. "But isn't he the cutest thing you've ever seen?"

The foursome emerges into the clearing and approaches the sisters' house. Rachel gasps and raises a hand to her mouth. A single sandal lies near an overturned stool. An overturned bucket rests beside a patch of wet ground. The basket of shellfish is scattered in the grass like drab Easter eggs.

"Someone has taken Bethany," Rachel cries. She stoops on one knee and calls to the yelping dog. "Draca, find Bethany!"

Draca sniffs the air, circles, and bolts away like a greyhound. Without waiting for the boys, Rachel chases the dog.

Jake says, "They've lied to us, called us witches, pushed us into a hole, and their dog hates us. So, we're going to help them, right?"

"Right!" Ethan agrees.

They sprint after the ragged girl, the ground sloping toward the sea. Branches claw their faces and briars grab their clothes. When they catch up, Rachel squats in the cover of blackberry bushes. Draca

hunkers at her side. When the boys peek through the branches, they see a thickset man swaggering toward the beach. Black hair dangles below an iron helmet. He wears baggy pants and chain mail. A sword hangs at his belt, and his right hand clutches a spear. Bethany, draped over his shoulder, struggles and pounds his back.

"Is that… Is that a Viking?" Spencer asks.

Rachel nods grimly. "A Northlander," she agrees.

"What incredible timing," Spencer says in an awed voice.

"Rachel, is today June 8?"

"I think so," she snaps. "What difference—"

"The date of the first Viking attack in Europe," Spencer tells his friends. "The day Norwegian raiders attacked the monastery on Holy Isle."

"The Vikings are not all on Holy Isle," Jake points out.

"He's well-armed," Ethan says, "and a born fighter. We need a plan."

"I can think of two ways Jake might handle this guy," Spencer says. "How about it, Jake the Jock? Do you want to be a wrestling champ or a quarterback hero?"

 TURN TO **PAGE 52**.

WHEN IN THE WORLD IS ETHAN CONWAY?

The Time Crashers have plopped into Lindisfarne on June 8, 793, the date of the first Viking attack on England. Do you feel like you came in on the middle of the story? Here's a timeline to get your bearings:

First do the math to figure out the date for each of the eight events given. Then fill in the date on the timeline below and draw a symbol above the line to represent that event.

June 8, 793
Viking attack
on Lindisfarne
(Holy Isle)

(1) Irish monk Columba brings Christianity to Scotland

Find the number of shekels in Numbers 3:50 and subtract 802.

(2) Irish monk Aidan founds the Monastery of Lindisfarne (Holy Isle)

Add 600 to the number of days in five weeks.

(3) *The Lindisfarne Gospels* are created

Find the number of ugly cows in Genesis 41:3. Multiply that number by 100.

(4) Vikings found the city of Dublin in Ireland

How many men were killed in 2 Kings 10:14? Multiply that number by 20.

(5) The monks abandon Lindisfarne because of continuing Viking attacks

How old was Jotham when he became King? (See 2 Chronicles 27:8.) Multiply that number by 35.

(6) Viking Erik the Red discovers Greenland

Add 81 to the number of iron chariots in Judges 4:3.

(7) Norway becomes a Christian country

Add 100 to the age of Mahalalel in Genesis 5:17.

(8) Christianity comes to the Viking lands of Iceland and Greenland.

How many gallons of olive oil are mentioned in Luke 16:6? Add 200 to that number.

ANSWERS: (1) 563 (2) 635 (3) 700 (4) 840 (5) 875 (6) 981 (7) 995 (8) 1,000

Football," Jake says. "That's my first love."

"I spotted this beside the path and thought it might be handy," Spencer explains. He tosses Jake a round rock the size of an orange. "How's your throwing arm?"

Jake hefts the rock, pitches it into the air.

"This is more like a baseball than a football," Jake says. "But I'm more than the football quarterback. I'm also the pitcher for the baseball team."

"When you finish polishing your trophies," Spencer says, "you can add another award to your bragging shelf: Jake Bradley—Girl Rescuer and Viking Basher."

Jake eyes the distance between himself and the Viking.

"I have to be sure to hit the Viking, not Bethany," Jake muses.

"Remember that long bomb you threw against Durrett last year?" Spencer asks. "The pass that took our team to the championships? That was nothing compared to this. Not to worry you, but a girl's life is at stake here, that's all."

Rachel's eyes are terrified and she hugs Draca close.

"This guy works best under pressure," Ethan whispers to her.

Across the clearing, the Viking lowers the wrestling girl to the ground, slaps her face, and slings her again over his shoulder. He strides off, heading into the trees.

"It's now or never," Spencer says. "Hero or heel? Whiner or winner? What's it going to be, Jake?"

The athlete pushes through the blackberry bushes and plants his feet. He flexes his throwing arm, makes a couple of practice motions, then hurls the rock. The stone arcs through the still air, rising, peaking, and falling smoothly. Jake stands with arms folded, a satisfied smile on his lips. Spencer, Ethan, and Rachel watch the missile with hypnotic fascination. From across the meadow comes a sharp

crack as the rock clunks the Viking's iron helmet. The raider drops to his knees and falls forward, pinning Bethany.

"Amazing! Astonishing! Astounding!" Spencer shouts, leaping on Jake's back. "You are the original action hero!"

"Right on his noggin," Ethan says. "Wow."

Jake blushes. "It's not as good as it looks," he admits. "I was aiming for his shoulder."

Draca leaps from Rachel's arms and dashes across the grass. The trio sprints behind the dog, arriving as Bethany wriggles free of the Viking's weight. While the sisters hug and cry, Jake asks, "Is he hurt bad?"

Spencer removes the Viking's dented helmet and feels his head. "He's got a lump. That's good. We don't want the swelling to turn inward."

The Viking opens his eyes and moans. Jake rolls the raider onto his stomach and drags his wrists together. He pitches a spool of dental floss to Spencer.

"You want me to clean his teeth?" Spencer asks.

"Tie his feet," Jake says rolling his eyes.

"Dental floss?" Spencer asks.

"Strong and tough like me," Jake explains. "And compact like you."

"Stay still," Jake commands, rolling the Viking onto his side after his hands and feet are tied. Icy blue eyes glare from the leathery face. The Viking's cheeks and chin are shaved, but a black moustache bristles beneath a thin, hooked nose.

"What's your name?" Jake asks.

"Frekis is my name," the Viking growls. "When I get loose I'll give you reason to remember it."

"Freaky, I feel bad about bombing you," Jake admits. "Then again you outweigh me by a hundred pounds, and you're packing more weapons than Iron Man."

"I hope the ants don't crawl into your ears and lay eggs," Spencer says, studying the Viking.

"Wiglaf!" Frekis bellows. "Wigl-a-a-a-a-a-f!"

Spencer crams his handkerchief into the Viking's mouth.

"Wiglaf?" Ethan asks. "Is that a name?"

Spencer nods. "I guess Freaky works with a buddy. It makes sense. One to scout the area and one to guard the land bridge. We'd

better go into stealth mode."

The girls guide the time travelers to the stone cross on the beach. Beside the water the girls rise on tiptoes, and each plants a kiss on Jake's reddening face.

"Woo-hoo!" Spencer jeers. "Jake the head-knocker and the heart-breaker."

Jake frowns. "You should be careful how you talk to a fellow holding a big axe and a very sharp sword."

Giggling, the girls trot from the beach. Before plunging into the trees, they wave and Draca barks.

From the woods behind them, Frekis shouts again. "Wiglaf! Wiglaf!"

"Your gag didn't work so well," Jake points out with satisfaction.

"I knew he'd spit it out," Spencer says. "We want his buddy heading into the woods and away from the beach."

"I should've known you had a plan," Jake grunts.

"I guess it's time to go home," Ethan decides.

"Shouldn't we look for your dad on the island?" Jake asks.

"There's no need," Spencer explains. "Dr. Conway never came here. After the rat failed to come safely home, Ethan's dad wouldn't take the chance. For all he knows, Frostbite the rat plopped into an avalanche or an atomic bomb blast. He's too smart to risk it."

"Dad couldn't know that Frostbite was carried off by Rachel the clam collector," Ethan says.

A prickling sensation tingles the skin of the three friends.

"Here comes the retrieval pulse," Ethan says, "right on schedule."

Jake looks wistfully at the Viking weapons. "You're sure I can't bring these back?"

"Afraid not," Ethan tells him. "The time machine won't bring anything from the past."

With a heave, Jake hurls the sword into the sea. With a plop it vanishes into the water. Grunting with effort, Jake flings the axe. It spins dizzily through the air. By the time it splashes into the waves, the three boys have disappeared.

THE END

 SEE EPILOGUE, PAGE 194.

Rachel, we understand why you feared us," Ethan tells the girl, "and we're not angry with you. But we don't have time for tea. Will you lead us back to the shore where you first saw us?"

"Of course," Rachel agrees. "Draca, come on."

The small dog rolls gleefully in the grass, his paws clawing at the sky. He rejoins the group, tail wagging exuberantly.

"Whoa!" Jake says, pinching his nose. "Whatever he rolled in, I'm glad I didn't step in it."

"Not again," groans Rachel. "You get a bath tonight, bad dog."

Rachel leads them toward the sea, casting wary glances at the foul-smelling Draca. They cross an open meadow and pass into a grove of trees. Rachel stops and points east.

"I have to get home so Bethany won't worry. The cross is that way," Rachel says. "Now what?"

"Good question." Ethan turns to his friends. "When Frostbite the rat didn't come home again, I don't think Dad would have followed him here. Then again, Dad can be stubborn. He might have come here just to find out what happened to his lab rat."

"Vikings," Jake says eagerly, pointing in the direction of Holy Isle.

"Ancient monks restoring western civilization," Spencer adds hopefully, also pointing east. "The chance of a lifetime."

 IF YOU THINK THE BOYS SHOULD RETURN HOME, TURN TO **PAGE 60**.

 IF YOU THINK THE BOYS SHOULD GO TO THE ISLAND, TURN TO **PAGE 66**.

Ethan chews his lower lip.

"This isn't a time travel vacation," he says at last. "Our job is to find Dad. I don't think he's on that island. The sooner we get home, the sooner we can make another trip."

"Okay," Spencer says, "but I don't have to like it."

The boys tell Rachel goodbye and walk toward the beach.

"I'm just saying this isn't much of an adventure," Spencer continues. "We come twelve hundred years into the past, crawl around in a muddy hole, and that's it."

"At least you won't be muddy when we get home," Ethan says. "Remember we can't bring anything back from the past, not even dirt. You'll be neat and clean when we reach the 21st Century."

"I guess that's something," Spencer agrees. "If I showed up

looking like this, my mother would be a lot scarier than a Viking. Even so, I was hoping for a little more danger, you know?"

In frustration, Spencer kicks a rotten log. Bits of pulpy wood fly into the air, and a flash of black-and-white streaks from beneath the log. The shape lunges at Spencer's ankle with lightning speed.

"Ouch!" Spencer cries, kicking at a snake about two feet long, with a black zigzag running along its back. The pale gray snake strikes again, once more biting through Spencer's thin sock. As the boy stomps at the snake, the animal escapes into the leaves with a faint rustle.

"That's more like it," Spencer says, flopping to the ground and clutching his ankle. His voice is light, but sweat beads his forehead. "Excitement and danger!"

Ethan rolls down his friend's sock and examines the tiny wounds.

"How much danger?" Jake asks.

"That serpent, my friends," Spencer beams, "is the nefarious European Adder, the only species of venomous snake in Britain. How awesome is that?"

"How dangerous is it?" Jake repeats, his tone urgent.

"The usual symptoms are severe swelling, nausea, and dizziness," Spencer explains.

"Spence, skip the Wikipedia," Ethan urges. "Are you going to be all right?"

"Most people survive the bite of the European Adder," Spencer says, "except victims who are allergic to the venom."

Ethan and Jake exchange fearful looks.

"Spencer, you have tons of allergies," Ethan says. "Do you think you're allergic to this snake's bite?"

"I think," Spencer mumbles, his words thick and cottony. "I shink ish poshible…"

Shivering wracks Spencer. His head falls backward.

Jake gingerly touches Spencer's ankle, swollen to the size of a grape fruit. "Should we try to suck out the poison?"

"That usually does more harm than good," Ethan says. He pulls out a handkerchief and ties it around Spencer's leg above the ankle. "Let's get him back to the cross."

Jake and Ethan get under Spencer's arms and lift him from the ground. Staggering unevenly under the load, they hurry down the trail toward the beach.

"He's in bad shape," Jake says, as they cross the rocky beach toward the stone cross. "Even if we get him home and call the life squad, I don't think he's going to make it."

"We won't need the rescue squad," Ethan says. "We just have to get him home."

They lower Spencer gently to the ground and sit him upright against the cross. Ethan loosens the tourniquet on his leg for a few minutes before retying the handkerchief.

"I don't understand," Jake says.

"The snake venom in his body," Ethan says, "It's part of the past, like the mud on our clothes. It won't return to the future with us."

"He'll still have two snake bites," Jake says, catching on, "but the poison will disappear from his body as soon as we leave. How long before the removal bus takes us out of here?"

"It better be soon," Ethan says.

The unconscious boy mumbles something, trembling  violently. Jake grabs Spencer's hand and closes his eyes.

"God, we're counting on you," Jake says. "You know how much we would miss Spencer with his big words and stupid facts. Please get us home and keep Spencer safe."

As Jake opens his eyes, a low humming throbs in the air. The boys feel the hairs rise on their arms and the back of their necks. Their skin tingles.

"Good timing on that prayer," Ethan says with relief.

"God's the one with good timing," Jake says.

"Amen," Spencer mutters.

A heartbeat later, the time travelers disappear. Two small blobs of sticky venom are left glistening on the rocks.

THE END

 SEE EPILOGUE, PAGE 194.

than grins. "Okay," he agrees. "We haven't been here long. We still have time for some exploring before we go home."

"You need to hurry," Rachel tells them. "The tide is rising, but there is still time for you to walk to the island."

"How can we walk to an island?" Ethan asks. "We can't walk on water."

"There is a causeway, a land bridge to Holy Isle," Rachel explains. "At low tide, people walk back and forth. At high tide the sea covers the causeway. From the standing cross, you will see the path. But hurry! You don't want the tide to catch you halfway to Lindisfarne."

Waving goodbye, the boys hurry to the beach. When they come out of the trees, they spot the cross and a dark-robed figure sitting beside it. As they tiptoe closer, they see that his chin rests on his chest and his eyes are closed.

"What do you make of that?" Ethan whispers.

 TURN TO PAGE 68.

The robed man's eyes spring open, and he gapes at the boys. An embarrassed smile lights his long face.

"I paused to pray for a moment before crossing to Holy Isle," he says, rising to his feet. "I must have fallen asleep."

Extending a bony hand, he says, "I am Brother Kelvyn."

After exchanging names and greetings, the monk says, "If you are going to Holy Isle, please walk with me. We have barely enough time before the tide cuts us off."

 TURN TO **PAGE 71**.

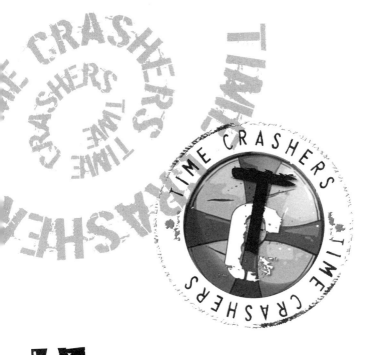

Although he can't read the verse, Ethan remembers the Bible taught him to have faith. If he keeps looking, there is hope of finding his father. Ethan decides to visit Holy Isle and ask for help from the monks. He believes his father would have gone to the island instead of the woods. After thanking Rachel, Ethan and his friends stride toward the sound of the sea.

A salty seawater smell drifts through the fog. Shells and stones crunch underfoot. As boys approach the water's edge, someone speaks from the thick mist.

"Who's there?" calls a deep, rich voice.

"Travelers," Ethan answers, "looking for Lindisfarne."

A man in dark robes emerges from the mist. He rushes at the boys with arms outstretched. Before they can turn or run, the man wraps them in a bear hug.

"I am Brother Kelvyn," he says heartily. "Please walk with me to Holy Isle."

"How can we walk to an island?" Ethan asks. "Won't we need a boat?"

Brother Kelvyn laughs. "Lindisfarne is a tidal island," he explains. "When the tide rolls in and the water is high, the sea separates the island from the mainland. When the tide retreats, a muddy road—a causeway—connects the island to the shore."

 SEE PAGE 71.

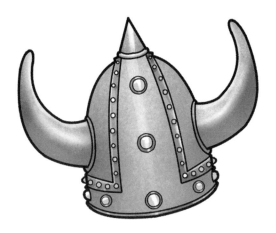

As they follow the monk through the clammy mist, Brother Kelvyn warns, "Don't wander off to the right or left. The water is cold and the currents are dangerous. Stay on the causeway with me and we'll soon be on Holy Isle."

Water laps on either side of the land bridge. Ethan studies Brother Kelvyn as they walk, a tall man with long arms and stork legs. In the movies, monks from long ago have heads shaved smooth on top with a fringe of hair on the side. Kelvyn's hair is the opposite. His head is shaved clean on the sides. Long hair on top sweeps back over his neck.

A breeze stirs the mist and the fog parts long enough to offer a glimpse of Holy Isle. Lindisfarne looks about three miles wide, mostly low, rolling land rising to a rocky hill in the center.

71

"It's good to be home," Brother Kelvyn says. "I've been gone a week gathering these."

With a grunt he lowers a heavy bag from his shoulder and opens the neck.

"Oak galls," Spencer says. He lifts a brown, wrinkled object the size of a ping-pong ball. "You make ink from these?"

"We create books in the monastery," Brother Kelvyn beams. "Our books are so beautifully lettered and decorated that you would think an angel had done the work. Have you come to study in our library?"

"A library," Jake says to Spencer. "Your dreams have come true."

"We're looking for another traveler," Ethan explains to their guide. He describes his father, watching the monk's face, but Kelvyn makes no sign of recognition.

"I will introduce you to the leader of our monastery, our Abbot," Brother Kelvyn promises. "Many pilgrims visit Holy Isle. If your friend has come here, the Abbot will know."

The monk rests the heavy bag on the damp causeway. As he catches his breath, he points toward different places on the island: vegetable gardens, a grove of walnut trees, a field of bee hives to provide honey, and a flock of black-and-white goats inside a pen.

A collection of small, simple buildings forms the monastery. Some are square stone structures roofed with a kind of hay called thatch. Other buildings are domes made from rocks skillfully piled on top of one another. They look like Eskimo igloos. These huts are the homes shared by the monks. In the center of the monastery grounds is a stone cross, similar to the one on the shore. Brother Kelvyn explains that the monks gather at the cross to pray and sing psalms.

"What a beautiful way to live," Spencer says.

A terrified shout suddenly shatters the peaceful mood. Someone on the island cries, "Dragons! Sea dragons!"

Blood drains from Brother Kelvyn's face. Through trembling lips, he whispers, "From the fury of the Northmen, good Lord deliver us." Abandoning the bag of oak galls, the long-legged monk runs for the island. "Go back!" he calls over his shoulder. "Hide in the woods!"

"I see them," Jake says, pointing into the sea mist.

Fierce dragon heads shred the fog, accompanied by the splashing of oars.

"Vikings," Spencer says. "Raiders from Norway."

Three Viking ships slither through the water. The boats are long and graceful, each with a snarling dragon carved on the prow. No wind fills the red sails, so the raiders row with long oars. Vikings leap into the surf, wading toward the defenseless monastery. They carry double-edged swords, long spears with iron points, and cruel battle-axes. Few of the Vikings wear armor except for iron helmets with long nose guards. As they splash toward shore, they bang weapons upon their wooden shields and scream battle cries.

"We're not soldiers," Ethan says grimly, "but we have to help the monks."

"Woo-hoo!" Jake shouts, pumping his fist in the air. "It's clobbering time!"

"Okay with me," Spencer agrees. "I want a better look at those Viking weapons."

"Come on," Ethan calls, hurrying after Brother Kelvyn. The fog thickens again, and the long-striding monk disappears in the mist. Even so, the causeway is easy to follow and soon the friends clamber onto Holy Isle.

Confusion sounds through the gray air: pounding feet, cries of fear and pain, and the thud of crashing weapons. Eye-stinging smoke mingles with the fog.

"The Vikings are burning the monastery!" Spencer cries.

Thatched roofs blaze with flames, painting patches of fog bright orange.

"What's worth stealing here?" Ethan asks. "What treasure do the Vikings hope to carry home?"

The bitter words have barely left Ethan's lips when a man staggers from the smoky fog. His hair is cut like Brother Kelvyn's. He wears the same style of dark robe. But this man is shorter, about Ethan's height. Blood mats his gray hair. He cradles a bundle wrapped in leather.

When the gasping monk sees the boys, his eyes widen.

"We won't hurt you," Spencer calls out. "We're not Norsemen."

The elderly monk stumbles to his knees, extending the bundle in trembling hands.

"Keep this," he pleads. "Protect it."

He collapses, face to the ground. The bundle lands at Jake's feet. Pursuing footsteps thud through the fog.

"Erik," rumbles a raspy voice. "This way, boy."

Spencer kneels by the monk, feeling for a pulse. The boy genius looks at Ethan and mouths one word: "Dead."

The time travelers have only seconds to escape the approaching Vikings. Should they obey the monk's dying wish? Or will the mysterious bundle slow them down and make them the target of greedy raiders?

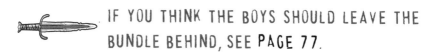

IF YOU THINK THE BOYS SHOULD LEAVE THE BUNDLE BEHIND, SEE **PAGE 77**.

IF YOU THINK THE BOYS SHOULD TAKE THE BUNDLE WITH THEM, TURN TO **PAGE 122**.

There's nothing more we can do for the old monk," Ethan says. "Whatever is in that bundle, it's not worth dying for."

Jake hesitates, but Ethan grabs his arm and pulls him into a run. Spencer falls in beside them and they race away, leaving the leather-wrapped bundle behind. They weave between bushes and boulders. The boys run single-file, Jake leading, Spencer bringing up the rear. Over the sound of their own pounding feet, they hear the pursuing Vikings.

Athletic Jake pulls further ahead of his friends without realizing. Ethan glances over his shoulder to check on Spencer. With one hand pressed to his chest, Spencer slows.

"His asthma!" Ethan says aloud. "He can't run in this damp air!"

Ethan feels a pang of panic as Jake pulls ahead and Spencer falls behind. He glances back again in time to see his friend trip and fall. Instead of leaping up, Spencer struggles to his hands and knees, panting for breath. Ethan races to help.

"Come on, buddy," Ethan says, stooping beside Spencer. "You can do it. A few more minutes and we'll lose them."

A shadow falls over the two boys.

"Aye, you've lost," says the red-bearded raider. "You've not lost us, but you've lost this race."

A young Viking with yellow braids accompanies the older raider. The Norwegian boy points his axe at Spencer who is fighting for breath. He turns to his companion and asks, "What's wrong with him, Harald?"

"He's sick," Ethan says.

"Then he's useless to us," red-bearded Harald says. "Kill him, Erik."

"Wait!" Ethan cries. "He has medicine. Give us a minute and you can return to camp with two captives instead of one."

Harald grunts and nods.

Spencer pulls an inhaler from his pocket, presses it to his lips, and draws in a shaky breath. In a few moments, he breathes more easily.

"Where's the other one?" Erik asks. "Your friend left you behind, didn't he? Ha! He's the smart one."

"On your feet," Harald orders, nudging Spencer with his sword. "Walk or we'll leave you to feed the ants and beetles."

"You'll have to leave us both here for the bugs," Ethan growls. "I'm not going without him."

"It's okay," Spencer says. "I'm doing better."

"Where are you taking us?" Ethan asks.

"To the ships," Harald says. "Then back to Norway where we'll sell you as slaves."

"You won't like Norway," Erik adds, "but it doesn't matter. You won't live through the first winter."

Jake looks back and sees no one. He slows, but Ethan doesn't appear. The athlete retraces the path, skulking in bushes and behind boulders. He spots his pals, marched along by the raiders. Ropes encircle his friends' necks, leashing them to the young Viking. The older one follows, sword drawn.

Jake wants to jump them, punching and kicking like a comic book hero, but that won't work. This will take planning. What would Spencer do? The Vikings are probably taking his friends back to their ships near the monastery. Jake circles wide, moving fast to get ahead of them. He spots two hardy bushes a few yards off the path, and an idea takes shape. From a vest pocket he pulls out what he needs to spring this trap. With preparations complete, Jake hides, hoping he has chosen the right place. After a few minutes, voices approach on the path.

"We have two slaves," Erik says. "One for me and one for you."

"You'll get what I give you and nothing more," Harald snorts. "Remember I'm the bear and you're the cub."

"I helped catch them," Erik argues.

Jake risks a peek through the branches that hide him.

"You're here because Ivar Forkbeard is your uncle," Harald sneers. "Ivar is our jarl, our chieftain, and he wants you to learn Viking ways. Fine. Watch and learn. But don't grab for loot or you'll get your hand slapped."

Heart racing, Jake steps out of hiding fifty yards from the path. "Hey!" he hollers. The startled Vikings jerk to a halt.

"You've only caught two of us," Jake jeers. "Don't you want to collect the complete set?"

Erik flings to Harald the ropes binding Ethan and Spencer.

"This one's mine," he says. He leaps from the path and sprints toward Jake. As he runs, he tugs the battle-axe from his belt.

Jake watches for a moment, smiling.

"Is that the best you've got?" Jake calls. He runs headlong into the stunted trees and brush, with Erik close behind.

"You should have hidden," Erik calls. "You're not as smart as I thought."

"We'll see about that," Jake says under his breath.

Bushes fly past in a blur. Jake searches for the right spot, past the thorny tree. There it is. The fine string stretched between two bushes is invisible, about a foot from the ground. He slows, letting Erik close the gap.

"My grandmother runs faster," Jake calls.

Jake clears the string and holds his breath, straining his ears for evidence that the plan has worked. Erik cries out in shock, and Jake hears a welcome thud as the Viking hits the ground.

Jake is on the yellow-haired boy in an instant. He wraps an arm around the boy's neck in a well-practiced wrestling hold. With his free hand, Jake wrenches the axe from the stunned Viking. The athlete drags Erik to his feet, pinning one of the boy's arms behind his back. Together they return to the path where Harald waits with his prisoners. The big Viking shakes his head in disgust.

"Little cub, next time leave the work to the bear," Harald says. He meets Jake's eyes and says, "Now what?"

"Now you give your sword to my friends and they use those ropes to wrap you up like a Christmas present," Jake says. He lifts the axe and presses the blade against Erik's throat.

"Go ahead," Harald says indifferently. He grips Spencer by the arm. "You kill that one; I kill this one." He jerks his head toward Erik. "He's too much trouble anyway."

"Do you want to go back to your chieftain, Ivar Forkbeard, and tell him that you got his nephew killed?" Jake asks.

Harald squints at Jake.

"You might really use that axe," he says. "Your friends are as soft as seal blubber, but you have the makings of a Viking."

With a resigned sigh, Harald drops his sword on the trail and extends his hands to Spencer.

"Not in front," Jake says. "Behind his back. Hobble his feet, too."

After Harald's hands are bound, Spencer connects his ankles with a short rope that allows only small steps. Ethan helps Jake tie Erik in the same fashion.

"Thanks for coming back," Spencer says.

"I owed you for all those times you've helped with my math homework," Jake says with a shrug. "Now we're even."

"Ha! In your dreams," Spencer answers. "You've saved my life once; I've saved your grade a hundred times."

"What do we do with our souvenir Vikings?" Ethan asks.

Jake folds his arms and studies the two prisoners.

"Let's deliver them to their buddies," Jake says. "It's time we taught these bullies a lesson."

As they hike across the island, the mist gradually lifts. By the

time they approach the shore where the Vikings have set up camp, a pale sun pierces the clouds. A layer of thick fog still hugs the sea, but the land is clear. Some Vikings sleep on the rocky ground, heads resting on rolled blankets, while others arm wrestle or trade stories. Cooking fires dot the beach. The smell of roasting meat drifts even to the hill where the time travelers have taken position. A cluster of monks huddle beside the water, captives bound for slave auctions. Ropes weave between their arms, tying them into one clump like a black jellyfish thrown up by the tide.

Spencer scans the camp. "No guards," he says. "They aren't expecting trouble."

"They aren't expecting us," Jake says. He shouts toward the beach, "Ivar Forkbeard! Your nephew wants to talk to you!"

Dozens of faces turn toward Jake, faces that twist in anger. Well-armed raiders climb toward the boys and their captives.

"Forkbeard!" Jake yells again. "Alone! Unless he's afraid to face three cubs!"

The charging Vikings pause, exchanging uncertain glances. On the beach, a tall man separates himself from a knot of warriors. A patch covers his left eye. Iron-gray hair hangs to his shoulders. His waist-length beard dangles in two braids like an upside-down V. His fur robe matches the shade of his hair.

"What a fur coat!" Spencer says. "A lot of bunnies died to

make that coat."

"Bunnies?" Erik spits on the ground. "They are wolf hides, each animal killed bare-handed by Uncle Ivar."

"Besides wolf-wrestling, does he have other hobbies?" Spencer asks. "Juggling porcupines? Gargling broken glass? Biting nails in two?"

The large man strides confidently up the hill. He stops a few paces from the group and rests his huge broadsword point down between his feet. The single black eye glances with distaste at Harald and Erik. He fixes Jake with a calculating gaze.

"I am Ivar Forkbeard, jarl of these men," he says. His voice is deep and raspy, like metal scraping metal. "What do you want for the boy?"

"I give you Harald Carrot-beard and Erik Girly-hair," Jake says, "and you free the monks."

A shaggy, gray eyebrow rises above the single icy eye.

"Twenty-five lives in exchange for two?" Forkbeard asks. "That is a poor trade."

"A few shivering monks swapped for your own flesh-and-blood," Jake counters. "It's a very good trade."

"I'm not fond of my sister," Forkbeard says. "She has a tongue like an adder. I only brought the boy along to shut up her nagging. I warned her Erik wasn't ready. I will enjoy telling her I was right."

"You'll stand before your men and let me run this axe across Erik's throat?" Jake demands.

"Idiots who get captured by beardless, unarmed boys," Forkbeard says evenly, "do not deserve pity."

Jake glances uncertainly at Ethan and Spencer.

"I offer a different deal," the jarl says, stroking his plaited beard with one massive hand. "I think you are followers of Jesus, like the monks."

"So?" Jake asks.

"I hear that Christians love each other," Forkbeard muses. "I wonder if it's true. I will free the monks if you three give yourselves up."

"Leave my friends out of it," Jake tells the Viking leader. "Take me and let the monks go."

Forkhead shakes his head. "Take it or leave it, boy."

"Count me in," Spencer says.

"Me, too," Ethan says. "If you think we can trust him."

"That's the problem," says Jake. "We know he's a killer and a thief. Is he a liar, too?"

 SEE PAGE 87.

"Okay," Jake tells the Viking chieftain. "I think you're a man who keeps his promises."

Jake lowers the axe from Erik's throat and cuts the young Viking's bonds. As soon as his hands are free, Erik turns on Jake, raising his fist. Forkbeard grabs his nephew's arm in a steely grip. Erik winces in pain.

"These whelps are my prisoners, not yours," Forkbeard growls.

Erik jerks free from his uncle and grabs his axe from Jake. He stalks down the hill, muttering under his breath. Pulling a razor-edged knife from his fur robe, Forkbeard slices the ropes that bind Harald's hands and feet.

"Put these three with the monks," he orders Harald, "unless they are more than you can handle."

"And the monks?" Harald asks.

"I'll free them," Forkbeard says, "but not until the ships are loaded. Let them earn their freedom with sweat."

Without another word, Harald pushes the boys down the hill to the beach, shoving whoever comes into his reach. At the waterline, he forces them to the damp earth beside the captives.

"Stay there," Harald orders them. "If I catch you wandering the camp, it will go hard with you."

 TURN TO PAGE 90.

THE MIGHTIEST WEAPON

What did Jesus teach us about dealing with people who don't like us? You can find out in the scrambled message below. Each word has the right letters, but they are out of order. Can you fix them? Unscrambling Jesus' words isn't too hard, but putting them into practice is tough!

VEOL RUYO MEENIES NAD YARP FRO SHOTE HOW CREESTUPE OUY, HATT OYU MYA EB DRENCHLI FO ORYU RETHAF NI HENAVE.

ANSWER: Love your enemies and pray for those who persecute you, that you may be children of your Father in heaven. (Matthew 5:44-45)

I'm going to check if any of these monks have seen Dad," Ethan tells his friends.

Jake studies the Vikings scattered across the camp. Some are working, sharpening weapons, repairing sails, stitching torn garments. But many are playing. In a circle of cheering men, two shirtless Vikings grapple in a wrestling match. Elsewhere, half a dozen men throw rocks at a target. Two men laugh and joke as they fight with blunt wooden swords. A few yards away, three warriors are intent on a game that involves moving pebbles around on a wooden board.

"These guys love their games," Jake says.

"I'd like to know more about that board game," Spencer says. "It looks like they're having fun."

 **TURN TO PAGE 93.**

VIKING FUN

What's your favorite board game? Checkers? Clue? Sorry?

The Vikings had a favorite called Tafl. They carried boards on their ships and played it all over the world. Even though it's hundreds of years old, it's still a fun game to play. See instructions on page 92.

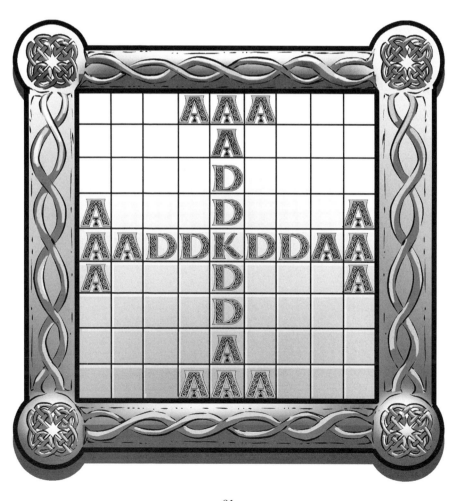

If you want to try it, make a paper board divided into nine rows of nine squares. One player will need a quarter and eight nickels for his Defenders. The other player will need sixteen pennies for his Attackers. Set the board up as shown on page 91: the quarter (the King) in the middle, the eight nickels (the Defenders) in a cross shape around the King, and the sixteen pennies (the Attackers) on the four edges of the board. Your board should look like the diagram when you begin to play.

Here are the rules. Toss a coin to see who moves first. Move one piece each turn. Any piece can move up and down or right and left (never diagonally) like the Rook in a game of chess. On your turn, you may move a piece as many spaces in a straight line as you wish, as long as you don't jump over another piece. Any piece can be captured if two enemy pieces surround it on opposite sides (above and below or right and left). The captured piece is removed from the board. To capture the King, the Attackers must surround the King on all four sides. If the King is captured, the Attackers win. If the King can reach the edge of the board, the Defenders win.

And no fair using swords or axes!

As Ethan moves among the monks, Jake says, "Okay, my plan to bring Erik and Harald back to camp didn't work, but I've got another plan to get us out of here."

"I was thinking about that, too," Spencer tells him. "I have an idea that should work without killing anyone."

"Hey," Jake says, "I wasn't going to hurt Erik. It was a bluff."

"Any word about your father?" Jake asks when Ethan returns.

Ethan shakes his head. "Anybody figured out a way to escape?"

Spencer and Jake look at each other and laugh.

"We have two brilliant plans," Jake says.

"Okay, let's hear them," Ethan says.

Each boy describes his plan, and after a few minutes Ethan says, "Either of those might work. How do we figure out which plan to follow?"

 IF YOU THINK THE BOYS SHOULD TRY JAKE'S PLAN, SEE **PAGE 95**.

 IF YOU THINK THE BOYS SHOULD CHOOSE SPENCER'S PLAN, TURN TO **PAGE 106**.

J ake turns to his friends. "I got us into this with my crazy idea of marching Erik and Harald back into the Viking camp," he says earnestly. "Give me the chance to get us out of this mess."

"None of this is your fault," Spencer says. "But if it means that much, you can have my vote.

Ethan nods. "Let's do it."

The three friends stride across the camp toward Forkbeard. The leader sits on a blanket-covered rock. He gnaws a hunk of mutton, grease dribbling onto his beard. When the sheep bone is clean, the jarl hurls it into a nearby fire where it lands with a spray of sparks. He wipes his hands on the front of his fur garment, belches, and turns his attention to the time travelers.

"What?" he growls.

"I've seen your men competing on the beach: wrestling, throwing rocks, playing games," Jake says. "Maybe one of your Vikings would compete with me in a foot race."

"I'm sure you have a prize in mind," Forkbeard says.

"If I win, my friends and I go free," Jake says.

"And if you lose?" Forkbeard presses him.

"You have the glory of victory," Jake says.

"Glory will not put salt on the table," Forkbeard says. "You'll have to offer something better than that."

"But we don't have anything to offer," Jake protests.

"Yes, we do," Ethan interrupts. "If you win, we will take you to a treasure you don't know about."

The dark eye ponders Ethan.

"Prove there is a treasure," Forkbeard demands.

"Prove you'll set us free," Ethan responds.

A grin brightens the jarl's grim face. "Fair enough," he says. Clapping his hands, he shouts, "Fetch Erik."

Within a few minutes, Erik arrives, his face darkening as he spots Ethan and his friends.

"These striplings shamed you, nephew," Forkbeard says. "They tricked you, took your weapon, and trussed you up like a salmon in a net. Now this one—" The chieftain points at Jake. "—says he can beat you in a foot race."

Erik glares at Jake. "He's fast when running away, but in a real race he'll see only my backside." Erik turns and slaps his behind in Jake's direction.

The onlooking Vikings roar their approval. Forkbeard silences the din with a raised hand.

"If you win," the leader tells Erik, "there will be treasure and a man's full share for you."

More roaring and shouting.

"If you lose, these three go free," Forkbeard intones. "And the story will be told for years to come how the soft southerners humiliated you twice in a single day. You will be Erik Stumblefoot for the rest of your life."

"I won't lose," Erik snaps. He wrenches the iron helmet from his head, unties his belt, and lays his weapons at Forkbeard's feet. "What's the course?"

Forkbeard points to a white rock five hundred yards down the shore. The rock slab, as large as an SUV, rests half on the beach, the other half washed by waves. The jarl draws the great sword from his belt and drags the point across the earth, digging a line in the sand.

"To that rock and back," Forkbeard instructs Erik and Jake. "The first one to cross this line wins. Understood?"

The runners nod and glare at each other. Jake shrugs out of his jacket and vest.

Forkbeard seizes a piece of bleached driftwood from the ground and tosses it high into the air. The stick spins lazily and turns earthward. The dry wood strikes the beach. Crack! The racers leap across the line.

Stones and shells strew the uneven beach. The race demands both speed and careful footing. For half the distance to the white rock, they run shoulder to shoulder. Jake gains ground, building a small lead. He is five feet ahead when he slaps the rock and spins to return. As he passes Erik, the young Viking extends his right arm and punches Jake in the stomach.

The Viking crowd cheers and whistles. The time traveler bends over and wraps both arms around his middle, staggering and stumbling. Erik hits the rock with one foot and pushes off in a smooth motion. In seconds he leaves Jake behind.

"That's not fair!" Spencer shouts at Forkbeard.

The jarl smiles wickedly. "Start here, end here," he says. "That's the only rule."

Erik widens the lead, but Jake catches his breath. He picks up speed, running fiercely. His feet rise and fall like pistons. His knees climb chest-high, arms hammering the air as if he might take flight.

"Go, Jake!" Ethan shouts, fists pumping.

"Make that cheater eat your dust," Spencer joins in.

Slowly, agonizingly, Jake nears Erik. He struggles to close the

last foot and then reaches the Viking boy's side. Erik's expression is unbelieving. For a moment they sprint side by side, as if glued together. Then Jake again takes the lead. With fifty yards left, Jake is three strides ahead.

Erik's face contorts with fear and rage. Barely slowing, the yellow-haired boy snatches a fist-sized stone from the rough beach. In a swift overhand motion, he launches the rock. The missile slams into Jake's left heel, and the athlete hits the ground like a sack of cement. He skids over the beach, stones ripping his hands and knees. Erik sails past the bleeding quarterback and crosses the finish line, basking in cheers and shouts.

By the time Ethan and Spencer reach their friend, Jake is on his feet, picking stones and shells from his palms. His pants are torn and bloody at the knees. He hobbles across the finish line, where Erik confronts him with a mocking grin.

"I won, Southlander," Erik crows.

Jake nods. "You won the race, but you didn't beat me," he says in a level voice. "I outran you. You know it. I know it. Everybody here knows it."

"Don't say that!" Erik shouts, spittle flying from his lips. "I beat you!"

"Keep shouting," Jake says, turning away. "Maybe you'll convince yourself."

Erik flings himself toward Jake's back, but an iron hand locks on his shoulder.

"Enough words," Forkbeard declares. "Our runner won; now

take us to the treasure. There had better be a treasure," he adds in a menacing voice.

"There's a treasure," Ethan promises. "Enough for every man here and plenty left over to take home to your families."

"Where is this abundant treasure?" Forkbeard asks. His eyes gleam with greed.

"On the mainland," Ethan tells him. "We can wait for the tide to turn and walk across the land bridge or we can go right now in your boats."

Forkbeard turns to the assembled Vikings. He shouts, "Shall we keep the treasure waiting?"

"No!" shouts the boisterous chorus. "Go now! Now!"

"Good," Ethan says. "Bring all three boats."

Forkbeard sizes him up with a sly look. "Two boats will be enough," he decides. "We'll leave a third of the men here to keep the monks company."

"Okay," Ethan says. "I didn't want anyone to be left out."

Although no wind fills the sail, the Vikings row efficiently, swinging the oars with an ease that shows long practice. In minutes the longboats near the mainland.

"A high cross stands at the end of the land bridge," Ethan tells Forkbeard. "Take us there."

The chieftain barks an order and the ship angles slightly, cutting through the foggy sea. In the mist, the outline of the stone cross appears, and the ship turns in that direction. Moments later the boats coast to stillness a few yards from the shore.

"Lead the way," Forkbeard orders Ethan.

The three friends drop over the side of the boat into waist-deep water. They slosh hurriedly toward the beach, eager to escape the bone-chilling sea. The Vikings splash ashore behind them and Ethan leads the band toward the stone cross.

"This map leads to the treasure," Ethan announces in a loud, clear voice, pointing to the cross. "If I teach you to read the map, you can find the treasure."

He steps to the backside of the cross, the side facing land.

"Here are carvings of animals," he says. A few of the Vikings drift around to watch as he points out strange, interwoven shapes. "The high-flying bird, the twisting snake, the galloping horse—all created by God. All of us are God's handiwork. People of the north and the south, monks and Vikings, we are all God's children."

"Do not preach Jesus to us," Forkbeard commands in a low, threatening voice.

"I am explaining the treasure map," Ethan says patiently. "If you want the treasure, you must understand the map."

A sudden twinge races up Ethan's spine and spreads across his skin like an electrical charge. The retrieval pulse is energizing. He glances at his friends to see if they feel it. Spencer nods.

"On this side of the cross are pictures of Jesus," Ethan hurries on, moving to the face of the cross overlooking the sea. He guesses at the meaning of some carvings. "There is Jesus healing a man who cannot walk. Over there Jesus raises a man from the dead. Here Jesus walks on the sea."

One of the Vikings calls out, "I'll take the sea-walker in my crew!" and the other Vikings laugh.

"And in the center of the cross is Jesus himself, reaching out for you," Ethan says. "He died for you and me, and he came back from the dead. He loves you and he wants to live in your heart. Someday he will bring his children to live with him forever in heaven."

"Enough!" Forkbeard roars. "Where is the treasure?"

"Right in front of you, Forkbeard!" Ethan says, his voice ringing out. "Jesus is the treasure, the greatest treasure of all."

Tiny pin-pricks stab the skin on his chest and back as the retrieval pulse grows stronger. A low humming throbs in the air, but the Vikings don't seem to hear it.

"Jorgen," Forkbeard calls into the crowd. "Do you have your bow?"

A barrel-chested Viking steps into the clearing, carrying a bow.

"Send this Jesus-lover to heaven," Forkbeard snarls.

"Ivar Forkbeard," Ethan says, pointing his finger at the chieftain. "Someday your people will love Jesus. It's only a matter of time before you forsake Odin and Thor. Lead the way! Carry the good news back to Norway."

Jorgen draws an arrow from a quiver hanging on his belt. He fits the arrow to his bowstring and takes aim at Ethan. He draws the string to his ear, muscles bulging in his arm. He holds the string taut, waiting for a sign from his jarl.

The humming rises in pitch and grows painfully loud for the three time travelers. It seems no one else can hear the noise. Spencer claps hands over his ears.

"Don't leave without the treasure," Ethan shouts to Forkbeard. "Don't go home without Jesus!"

Forkbeard looks at Jorgen and makes a slicing motion with one hand. The archer releases his grip. The string twangs and the arrow leaps from the bow.

But Jorgen's target is gone. The time travelers have vanished. The arrow strikes the cross and shatters into splinters. Forkbeard howls his rage to the sky. But Erik, the young Viking boy, stares at the cross in awe. He studies the face of Jesus. He meets the loving eyes. And Erik wonders if Ethan is right about the treasure.

THE END

 SEE EPILOGUE **PAGE 194**.

know my plan will work," Spencer insists. "And it will put Forkbeard in his place without anyone getting hurt."

"That's good enough for me," Jake says. "If Spencer Strong-Head says it will work, I believe him."

"Strong-Head?" Spencer asks.

"I like these Viking names," Jake admits.

"Okay, Spencer, you're on," Ethan says.

The three friends climb to their feet and walk across the camp toward Forkbeard. The leader sits on a blanket-draped rock, gnawing a hunk of mutton. When he has chewed the bone clean, the jarl pitches it into a nearby fire. He cleans his hands on his wolf-skin garment, belches, and turns to the time travelers.

"Yes?" he says, his tone sharper than a blade.

"A riddle game for our freedom," Spencer answers in a loud voice. Several faces turn toward him. A few Vikings drift closer to hear the challenge. "Between you and me, Forkbeard."

Forkbeard ponders Spencer with a slight smile.

"I'm smarter than you, and I want to prove it," Spencer says bluntly.

Some of the nearby Vikings gasp and glance fearfully at their jarl.

"I have nothing to prove," Forkbeard says as his smile vanishes.

"You do now," Spencer says. "Your men heard me insult you. If you refuse to play, they'll know you are afraid."

"Afraid of a beardless stripling?" Forkbeard asks. "Since you challenge me, I go first. If you can answer my riddle, it's your turn. We go back and forth until someone is stumped. If you win, you take your freedom. If I win, I take your head. Do you agree?"

"No way!" Ethan shouts. "Don't do it, Spence!"

Spencer swallows hard. "Let's hear your first riddle."

The crowd of Vikings has grown, and now most of the camp has gathered to witness the riddle game.

Forkbeard cocks his head and smiles at Spencer. "I'll start with

an easy one. *Wonder on the wave, water becomes stone. What am I?*"

"That's a gimme," Spencer says. "The answer is ice on a lake."

Forkbeard nods. "Your turn."

"If a man carried my burden, he would break his back. I am not rich, but I leave silver in my track," Spencer recites.

"I hope you can do better than that," Forkbeard snaps. "A snail carries his own house, but a man cannot do as much."

Spencer spreads his hands, nods, and waits for the next riddle. Forkbeard rubs a crooked finger along one hairy cheek, deep in thought. "Ah," he says. "Try your wit on this one:

I'm wounded by iron and scarred by sword, but I never bleed.

Spears and sharp-edged swords bite into me, but I never weep.

I protect others, but no one protects me.

I receive death blows from fierce enemies, but no one comes to help me."

"What receives more blows—and less help—than a warrior's shield?" Spencer asks with a faint smile. Without waiting for Forkbeard to approve his answer, Spencer plunges into the next puzzle. *"I have no top or bottom, yet I can hold flesh, blood, and bones all at the same time."*

Forkbeard screws up his face in concentration. He absent-mindedly twists a gold ring on his middle finger, and suddenly his expression brightens. "A ring! A ring holds flesh, blood, and bone."

Spencer nods, disappointment written on his face.

"Remember I claim your head if you lose," Forkbeard reminds Spencer. "Keep that in mind as you work on this one. *They take me captive and cut off my head. They bite my body. I do no harm to anyone unless they cut me first. Then I soon make them cry.*"

Spencer paces back and forth, pondering the riddle. Having

had no lunch or dinner, Spencer's stomach growls, and the rumbling wakes his brain. "An onion!" he says. "Now here's one for you: *As long as I live, I eat; but when I drink, I die.*"

Forkbeard rubs his chin and stares into the distance. Minutes tick by, the crowd utterly silent. A piece of pine pops in the nearby fire and sparks swirl skyward. Forkbeard glances toward the burning sticks. He grins. "A fire is always eating," he says, "but dares not take a drink."

The minutes become an hour, then two hours, as the puzzles bounce back and forth.

"*What swallows flesh and blood at night and spits them out in the morning?*"

"*What musician invites death every time he sings to you?*"

"*How can you add ten to ten and still have ten?*"

"*What is full of holes, yet holds water?*"

"*It belongs to you alone, but it is used more by your friends?*"

 TURN TO **PAGE 113**.

 TURN TO NEXT PAGE TO SOLVE THE RIDDLES.

BRAIN BURNERS

Riddles are a workout for your brain. Are your brain cells smoking as you try to figure these out? If there are any you can't solve, the answers are given here in number code. 1 is A, 2 is B and so on. Fire up those mental muscles!

What swallows flesh and blood at night and spits them out in the morning?
ANSWER: 1   8-15-21-19-5

What musician invites death every time he sings to you?
ANSWER: 1   13-15-19-17-21-9-20-15

How can you add ten to ten and still have ten?
ANSWER: 16-21-20   15-14   7-12-15-22-5-19

What is full of holes, yet holds water?
ANSWER: 1   19-16-15-14-7-5

It belongs to you alone, but it is used more by your friends?
ANSWER: 25-15-21-18   14-1-13-5

a house, a mosquito, put on gloves, a sponge, your name
ANSWERS:

Some puzzles are easy, some tricky, but neither riddler can stump his opponent. Both Spencer and Forkbeard grow tired and hoarse as they throw riddles at each other. At length, the Viking chief rises and stretches. He says, "You are wise beyond your years, pup, but I tire of this game. I declare this match a draw, no winner, no loser. You keep your head, and I keep you."

"You gave the first riddle," Spencer says. "I should give the last."

"Fair is fair," Forkbeard agrees. He settles back to his seat. "One final riddle."

"The more you take, the more you leave behind," Spencer says.

Forkbeard squints his single eye. His lips move as he repeats the riddle under his breath. Waves lap the shore, counting slowly as the jarl wrestles with the riddle. As Forkbeard's expression grows darker, Spencer's brightens with hope. Shoulders slumped, scowling fiercely, the Viking leader admits, "I cannot solve it. What is the answer?"

"*The more you take, the more you leave behind,*" Spencer repeats. "The answer is footsteps."

Ethan slaps Spencer on the back with a whoop. Jakes grabs him in a bear hug and heaves him off the ground, spinning in a circle.

When Spencer has his feet back on the beach, he turns to Forkbeard. "A good game," Spencer tells the chieftain. "Now my friends and I will be making footsteps out of your camp."

"Well played," Forkbeard admits. "You are free to go, and I give you one hour safe passage before my men come after you."

"You said we could have our freedom!" Spencer protests.

"But I never promised you could keep it," Forkbeard smirks. "There are many ways to play the riddle game, boy, and sometimes the winner is the loser."

"They ought to call you Forktongue, you lousy—" Jake snarls.

"Never mind, big guy," Spencer says, grabbing his arm. "Let's make the most of our time."

Grumbling and muttering, Jake falls into a jog beside Ethan and Spencer.

"Back to the causeway?" Spencer asks.

"We've got to reach that stone cross if we hope to get home,"

Ethan agrees.

As they climb a small hill, they look down toward the land bridge—but it isn't there. The afternoon sunlight shows only misty water.

"The tide has covered the causeway," Spencer sputters.

Ethan studies the shoreline. Glistening rocks and bits of seaweed lie well above the water. "The tide's going out," he decides. "We can wait while the causeway opens."

"In less than an hour," Jake warns, "the braidy bunch will be after us."

"Yeah," Spencer agrees, "and Forkbeard wasn't wearing a Timex. Maybe his hour has only forty minutes."

"We should wait a while," Jake says. "That's cold water, and it's a long way to the mainland."

He meets Ethan's eyes. His expression shows worry about Spencer's asthma.

"Good idea," Ethan agrees. He moves a few yards down the hill so they cannot be seen from the Viking camp. He settles on the ground with a tired sigh. "I need a breather."

"Maybe the Vikings won't come after us," Spencer says, flopping beside him.

Jake laughs.

"No, they won't come after *us*," the athlete tells his friend.

"They'll come after *you*. You are Number One on Forkbeard's hate list right now."

"It was a fair match," Spencer insists.

"That doesn't matter. You embarrassed him in front of his men," Jake says. "Old One-eye wants to make you his personal slave boy. If he catches you, you'll spend the rest of your life polishing his sword, braiding his beard, and picking bugs out of his hair."

"That's great job security," Spencer says. "Do I get weekends off?"

As they swap jokes, the waterline recedes. Wave by wave, the breach grows wider and small sandbars dot the sea along the path of the land bridge.

"Do you think it's been an hour yet?" Ethan asks.

Jake crawls to the hilltop and pokes his head up.

"The Vikings think so," Jake says. "A dozen of them are gathering up their weapons. Yep, here they come."

"A dozen of them?" Spencer asks.

"They figure it will take at least eleven to capture me," Jake declares. "That leaves Erik to grab you two."

"Do you know what the front bike wheel said to the back wheel?" Ethan asks.

"Yeah," Spencer says. "Let's roll!"

They run down the hill. Spencer pauses at the water's edge long enough to use his inhaler, and they leap into the shallows. Here and there they wade through waist-high water, but more often they run across sandy flats and stretches of soft mud. Muddy ooze sucks at their shoes, rising above their ankles. They struggle on, raising their filthy feet with plopping noises.

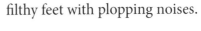

Behind them, the Viking band reaches the shore and plunges after the runaways. The shouts and jeers of the raiders ring out over the causeway. Glancing over his shoulder, Jake says, "We don't have much of a lead on them."

"Don't worry," Spencer pants. "We have an advantage. They're bigger than us and they're carrying swords and axes."

"That sounds like their advantage," Jake says.

"Not in the mud," Spencer assures him.

Jake risks another look back.

"You're right!" he says. "They're bogging down, sinking to their knees."

"Sure," Spencer tells him. "They outweigh us, and those iron weapons are heavy. We're going to leave them behind."

"Not all of them," Jake observes. "Erik's closing the gap."

"Three of us and one of him," Ethan calls. "No problem."

"Maybe, maybe not," Spencer says. "When is two greater than three?"

"Enough with the riddles already," Jake moans.

"One Viking plus one axe is greater than three unarmed time travelers," Spencer says.

"No wonder I hate math," Jake says.

"This math problem just got more complicated," Ethan exclaims. "There's a Viking on the mainland waiting for us."

A bear-like figure stands at the end of the land bridge, holding a sword in one hand and a huge battle-axe in the other. He peers through the mist at the approaching runaways.

"Forkbeard must have posted a guard to capture anyone escaping from the island," Spencer decides. "That Forkbeard is no dummy."

"Great! You can start a Forkbeard Fan Club if we live through this," Jake snaps, "but what do we do now?"

"Scatter," Ethan orders. "Get to the cross no matter what."

With Erik on their heels and the other Viking waiting, the boys split up as soon as they near the shore, Jake cutting to the right and Ethan and Spencer running left. Erik dives for Jake, but falls short, catching a foot in the face. The Viking guard drops his weapons and lunges for Ethan and Spencer, grabbing Spencer by the shirt.

Jake and Ethan stop a few paces from the cross, watching helplessly as Spencer struggles in the grip of the burly guard.

Erik leaps to his feet, spitting sand, and shouts, "These prisoners are mine, Wiglaf."

"Says who?" Wiglaf growls.

"I chased them all the way here," Erik says.

"And I caught them," Wiglaf points out.

Erik, red-faced and furious, stalks toward the larger Viking, still gripping the battle-axe. The guard hurls Spencer to the ground and seizes his own weapons. Spencer runs across the beach, joining his friends beside the great, stone cross.

Wiglaf brandishes his axe at Erik and says, "Don't lose your head, boy, or you might lose your head."

"Stop it!" Ethan shouts. He feels a familiar sting electrify his skin as the retrieval pulse energizes. "There's nothing to fight over. We're nobody's prisoners. We're going home now, and carving each other up won't change that."

The guard grins and shakes his shaggy head.

"They are as crazy as you, Erik," Wiglaf says. "Let's show them who's in charge."

Both Vikings stride across the sand. Weapons in hand, they confront the time travelers at the foot of the cross. A low humming rises in Ethan's ears as throbbing energy raises goose bumps on his arms and hands.

Leveling his sword at Ethan, Wiglaf demands, "Now what do you have to say?"

"Just one thing," Ethan tells him. "Jesus loves you."

With a faint sound, like an inhaled breath, the three boys vanish. Erik and Wiglaf stare at each other in wonder. Behind them, shouting Vikings struggle across the land bridge, stamping mud-caked feet on the rocky shore.

"Where are they?" red-bearded Harald demands. "Where are the runaways?"

"They…" Wiglaf wags his sword at the cross. "They…"

"They what?" Harald roars.

"They…" Wiglaf repeats, eyes wild and round.

"They went home," Erik says.

THE END

 SEE EPILOGUE **PAGE 194.**

ake grabs the leather-wrapped package.

"Let those Vikings try to snatch this," he warns.

"Be careful what you wish for!" Spencer says as two attackers appear from the mist.

The Vikings step over the lifeless monk and turn their cold eyes on the boys. One raider has a tangled, orange beard hanging over a broad chest. He clutches a spear dripping with blood. The other Norwegian is young, about Ethan's size. Yellow braids dangle from beneath his iron helmet. He carries a battle-axe in one hand and a circular shield in the other.

Ethan glances at his friends. Spencer stares with wide eyes, either terrified or making mental notes for an A+ Vikings report for Mr. Nutt's history class. Jake leans forward in a wrestler's stance.

The monk's package is nowhere in sight.

The bearded Viking laughs and hurls his spear at Ethan. Time slows as the weapon slices through the air. Ethan is frozen by shock, his feet rooted to the earth, like a rabbit waiting for the claws of a hawk.

"No!" Jake cries.

The athlete leaps between Ethan and the fire-haired Viking. Arms spread wide, fists clinched, Jake shouts defiantly. His body shields Ethan from the spear. The deadly iron point slams into Jake, piercing his jacket, sinking inches deep.

The weight of the spear knocks Jake off his feet. He lands on his back, the breath whooshing from his lungs. The spear sticks straight up from his belly. The bearded Viking plants a muddy boot on Jake's shoulder and grabs the spear. He pulls hard, staggering back when the point jerks free. Jake lies on the damp grass coughing, clutching at the torn and bloody hole in his jacket. He tries to sit up, falls to his side, and rolls over on the trampled ground.

Should Ethan and Spencer run away or should they stay and fight? What would Jake want them to do?

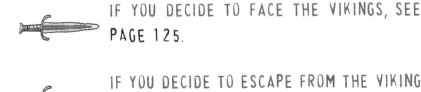

IF YOU DECIDE TO FACE THE VIKINGS, SEE PAGE 125.

IF YOU DECIDE TO ESCAPE FROM THE VIKING ATTACK, TURN TO PAGE 131.

Standing over Jake's still body, blood pounds in Ethan's temples. Boiling with anger, he throws himself at the red-bearded killer. The Viking raises a muscled arm and hits Ethan with the shaft of the spear. As the wood slams his head, the world spins around. Ethan remains upright only because Spencer grabs his arm. By the time Ethan's head clears, the older Viking points the spear at his belly and the younger raider holds his axe over Spencer's head.

"White flag," Spencer says. "We capitulate. Give up. Submit. Surrender. Concede. Sign a treaty. Whatever. Now take us to your leader."

"Leave the big bellied one," the bearded warrior grunts, jerking his head at Jake's still form. "He's finished."

"Harald, can we sell these two as slaves?" the boy asks.

The older Viking, Harald, shrugs. "The black one is small and weak, Erik. We'll let Forkbeard decide."

 IF YOU THINK ETHAN AND SPENCER SHOULD TRY TO ESCAPE, SEE **PAGE 127.**

IF YOU THINK IT IS BETTER FOR THEM TO GO WITH THE VIKINGS TO THEIR CAMP, TURN TO **PAGE 130.**

than leads the Vikings a few steps away from Jake and turns to stare Harald in the eye.

"We're not going with you," Ethan says.

"Because you want to die here?" Harald asks, a wicked grin parting the tangle of his beard.

"No," Ethan says, "because we know something you don't know."

Behind Harald, Jake lifts a stone in both hands and smashes it on the big Viking's helmet. Like a cartoon character, Harald's eyes cross and he crumples to the earth, his dented helmet rolling across the grass. In the same moment, Spencer leaps at the yellow-haired boy. They tumble in a knot of waving arms and kicking legs. Jake and Ethan peel them apart. They tie the struggling boy's hands and feet together, using his own belt as a rope.

"How's that for small and weak?" Spencer says, pushing his face close to Erik's.

"Nice tackle, Bookworm," Jake says and slaps his friend on the back.

"How come you're not dead?" Spencer asks, squinting suspiciously at his friend.

"I'll explain on the way," Jake assures him, "but we'd better get moving before Robin Redbeard wakes up."

The helpless Erik looks up at them in surprise. "Aren't you going to kill us?" he asks.

"We aren't killers," Ethan tells him. He points toward a tall, stone cross lit by flickering flames. "You can thank Jesus for that."

"I don't believe in Jesus." Erik spits the words.

"But we do," Jake says.

he three friends leave the Vikings behind. As they move through the brush, Spencer eyes Jake. "I thought you were a goner."

"Sorry to ruin the funeral plans," Jake says, opening his baggy jacket and pulling the monk's leather-wrapped package from inside. "I didn't have much time to hide it, and this seemed like the best place. It turned out to be my own personal spear-proof vest."

Spencer slams a palm against his forehead. "So that's why the Viking thought you had a big belly."

"The blood on the spear splashed on Jake's coat," Ethan says, "making it look like he was really stabbed."

"Let's take a look at the thing that saved my life," Jake says.

 TURN TO **PAGE 164**.

Tie them," Harald orders.

Erik draws rope from a leather bag on his belt. He makes a loop on each end of the rope, tied with a slip knot, and snugs the nooses around the necks of the time travelers. If they try to run, the loops will draw tight and strangle them. He holds the middle of the rope in a tight grip, driving the boys like leashed dogs before him. Spencer stares over his shoulder until Jake's body is out of sight.

 TURN TO **PAGE 141.**

ake lifts his head and fixes his eyes on Ethan. "See you in history," he says earnestly. "In *history*."

His body goes limp.

Ethan stares at his motionless friend. Is there any chance to save Jake? Ethan yanks Spencer into a run. The two sprint away from the fallen Jake and the angry Vikings.

"Save the gold!" Ethan shouts. He whispers to Spencer, "That should get their attention!"

The smaller boy nods and calls over his shoulder, "Beat them to the treasure."

Behind them, the older Viking yells, "Catch them, Erik!"

The Norse raiders race after the boys. They keep pace in spite of the weight of their weapons and helmets. At Ethan's side, Spencer wheezes, taking shallow, rattling breaths.

"My asthma," Spencer pants. "Dampness. *Ahuh!* Smoke. Getting—*Ahuh!*—to me."

A stand of small trees and heavy bushes appears as the boys round a bend in the path. As if sliding into third base, Ethan buries himself feet first under a thicket of brush. Spencer lands beside him, his breathing harsh.

"Leave me," he pants. "I'm—*Ahuh!*—slowing you down."

"Maybe they'll run past us," Ethan whispers.

Instead, the raiders slow as they approach the saplings and bushes. They peer this way and that. Spencer buries his mouth in the crook of his arm to muffle his labored breath. Ethan wonders if he should stay with Spencer or try to lead the pursuers away in the fog.

As the Vikings turn, straining their ears and eyes, Ethan makes a quick decision.

 IF YOU THINK ETHAN SHOULD STAY WITH SPENCER, SEE PAGE 133.

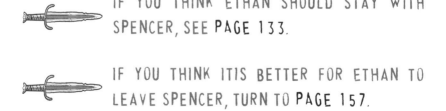 IF YOU THINK IT IS BETTER FOR ETHAN TO LEAVE SPENCER, TURN TO PAGE 157.

than loves Spencer like a brother, but what is the best way to show that love? Ethan grips his friend's arm and whispers, "I'm going to stick with you like ketchup on a white shirt. If the Vikings find us, we'll face them together."

Spencer nods, still panting into the crook of his arm. Ethan squashes himself flatter against the wet grass and moldy leaves beneath the bushes. The decaying leaves give off a stench of mildew, the odor filling Ethan's nose. A sneeze tickles inside his head. He scrunches his face tight, fighting the sneeze, but it wiggles like a feather in his nostrils.

"They've slipped away, Harald," the Viking boy says to his older companion.

Harald shakes his head emphatically, his beard fluttering like a ragged flag. "Be still, Erik," the Viking commands. "Use your ears, pup, not your mouth."

The sneeze swells inside Ethan's head, like a balloon getting closer and closer to popping.

"Ah," Ethan breathes. "Ah…"

Spencer looks at his friend and his eyes grow as large as Frisbees.

"Ah…"

Ethan clamps two fingers over his nose.

"Ah-ah—"

"Maybe you're right," Harald concedes. "I think we've lost—"

"CHOO!"

The sneeze explodes, louder than a firecracker in church.

"Over there," the Viking boy shouts, pointing toward their hiding place.

Now what?

IF YOU THINK ETHAN AND SPENCER SHOULD TRY AGAIN TO ESCAPE, SEE **PAGE 135**.

IF YOU THINK ETHAN AND SPENCER SHOULD SURRENDER TO THE VIKINGS, TURN TO **PAGE 137**.

than and Spencer lock eyes.

"Run?" Ethan whispers.

Spencer nods once and scrambles from the cover of the bush, Ethan close behind him.

"No more of this game," the big Viking Harald shouts after them. "Stop or I'll stop you!"

Ethan pulls alongside Spencer, pointing ahead to a grove of trees.

"If we can get into those trees, we might throw them off," Ethan says.

Spencer nods once; he doesn't have enough breath to answer. Without warning, the smaller boy stumbles and sprawls. Thinking his friend has tripped, Ethan grabs for his hand. An ugly spear protrudes from Spencer's back and a red stain spreads across his jacket.

"Oh, no," Ethan sobs.

A whistling sound slices through the air. Ethan looks up in time to see the battle-axe spinning toward him. A sudden weight crashes into Ethan's chest. The impact smashes him to the cold ground. Warm wetness soaks his chest.

The red-bearded Viking stands over the boys, looking down in disgust.

"I could have sold you for gold," he said. "Now you're supper for the worms."

Ethan tries to answer. Breath rattles in his throat. He closes his eyes for the last time.

THE END

YOU DON'T LIKE THIS ENDING?

DO YOU WISH ETHAN HAD MADE OTHER CHOICES?
GOOD NEWS! YOU HAVE A TIME MACHINE. GO BACK AND
DO IT DIFFERENTLY. THE FINAL ENDING IS UP TO YOU.

than and Spencer lock eyes.

"Run?" Ethan whispers.

"Can't—*Ahuh! Ahuh!*" Spencer wheezes. "You—*Ahuh!*—go on."

"No way," Ethan says. "Remember? I'm sticking with you like stink on gym socks. Like peanut butter on the roof of your mouth."

"Like chewing gum—*Ahuh!*—on a summer sidewalk," Spencer says with a grin.

"Like dog poop on track shoes," Ethan adds with finality.

Two powerful hands reach into the bushes, grabbing each boy by an ankle, and dragging them into the open.

"You found us fair and square," Ethan says, brushing leaves and sticks from his clothing. "Now we'll cover our eyes and count to one hundred while you hide."

The raider grabs the front of Ethan's jacket in one hairy hand and hoists him off the ground. He thrusts his face so close to the time traveler that the wild, red beard scratches Ethan's chin.

"Are you crazy?" Harald asks.

"Some of my friends think so," Ethan admits. "Now I have a question for you. Do Vikings know about mouthwash?"

Harald rams Ethan back to the ground with bone-jarring strength. "This one has spirit," the Viking says. "He'll bring a good price on the slave block."

"What about the shrimpy one?" Erik, the Viking boy, asks.

"No meat on his bones," Harald says, eyeing Spencer. "But

have you ever seen a person so dark-skinned? I might keep him for myself. If he were serving at my table, the whole town would be knocking on my door."

"He's half mine," Erik challenges.

With practiced ease, Harald loops a rope around each boy's neck, a slipknot choker.

"Forkbeard will judge that," Harald grunts. "When you do a man's work, you get a man's share."

Harald and Erik prod their prisoners across the island. As they wind through the fields, Spencer uses his inhaler and soon breathes steadily.

TURN TO **PAGE 141**.

I'M GLUE, SO ARE YOU.

Ethan and Spencer are sticking together even when things are tough. The Bible teaches that friends like that are a real blessing: A friend loves at all times, and a brother is born for a time of adversity. (Proverbs 17:17).

Have you ever heard of the friendship knot? This knot ties two pieces of rope together and the harder you try to pull them apart, the tighter the knot becomes. That's how real friendship works. The harder life becomes, the tighter a real friend hangs on. Do you have people like that in your life?

If you'd like to make a friendship knot, get two pieces of cord or rope. You can even use shoelaces if you can't find other string. Then follow the drawings. When you've finished, try to pull the strings apart and see how the knot gets stronger!

As Ethan and Spencer are marched over Lindisfarne, the mist slowly clears. After a few minutes, the ground slopes downward and the smell of the sea drifts through the air. Laughter and shouts mingle with the sound of ocean waves.

Topping a slight rise, the time travelers spot the beach. Although blankets of gray fog hug the sea, the boys view the shore clearly. Cooking fires and milling Norwegians dot the rocky seaside. Twenty or twenty-five monks sit huddled together near the waterline, their arms tied with intertwining ropes. Some are wounded and blood-stained. All appear cold and exhausted. A few yards away, the three dragon boats bob in the shallows.

Further from the water, two shirtless Vikings are wrestling. A circle of spectators cheers and razzes them. As the captive boys trudge nearer, one wrestler topples the other and pins his back to the earth. A roar rises from the crowd. The victorious Viking leaps to his feet, dancing wildly.

"Well done!" calls a tall man wrapped in fur. "A gold ring for the winner…" He flips a shiny piece of jewelry to the dancing Viking. "And a silver ring for the loser." The beaten wrestler plucks a second bit of bright metal from the air.

The onlookers pound sword handles against their shields, shouting, "Ring Giver! Ring Giver! Hail Ivar Forkbeard! Hail the Ring Giver!"

The tall man notices Harald and Erik leading the captured time travelers. He seats himself on a blanket-draped rock, and beckons the prisoners. The Viking chief has a fierce, chiseled face and a gray beard split into two braids that brush his belt. A patch hides one eye. The other eye studies the captives with a stare as black and cold as a raven's gaze.

"Two more slaves," Harald announces, slipping the ropes from the necks of Ethan and Spencer.

"More like two lambs," Ivar Forkbeard announces. Laughter ripples through the crowd. "One black sheep and one white."

"They are half mine," Erik tells the chieftain. "I shared the chase."

"We'll see," the one-eyed man says, stroking the length of his twin beards. "For now, bind them and put them with the—" The jarl, the Viking chieftain, breaks off. He cocks his head and studies Erik with amazement. A red dot has appeared on the boy's forehead. The dot moves in a tiny circle, then flits to Erik's chest. It traces a wider circle on the boy's leather shirt.

"By the nine worlds," Forkbeard rumbles. "What magic is this?"

The scarlet dot flicks from Erik to Ethan, sitting immobile over the time traveler's heart. Ethan and Spencer exchange glances.

"Explain this sorcery," the jarl demands of Ethan. He draws a long knife from the folds of his fur robe. "And do not lie to me."

"Tell him," Spencer says to Ethan. "No treasure is worth dying for."

"It is, uh, the eye of, uh, Odin," Ethan tells Forkbeard.

"That's right," Spencer agrees, "the eye of Odin."

"A sign given to the bravest warriors," Ethan adds.

"The dark one spoke of treasure," Forkbeard says, moving the knife close to the glowing red dot on Ethan's chest.

"Yes, Odin's eye leads to gold," Ethan admits.

"Why have I never heard of this?" asks the jarl, squinting suspiciously.

"We are from a faraway place," Spencer tells him. "We know many secrets and mysteries."

The ruby dot leaps from Ethan's jacket to a boulder on the beach, then to another rock a few yards inland.

"Follow!" Ivar Forkbeard roars. "Follow the eye of Odin!"

As the Vikings gather their weapons, the chieftain turns to young Erik.

"You remain here and watch the prisoners," he orders. "Since you claim a share in the slaves, you can have a share in guarding them."

Erik opens his mouth to protest, but a single glance from Forkbeard's dark eye changes the boy's mind.

"I'll guard them well, my jarl," Erik mumbles.

As the band of shouting Vikings chase the dancing red dot into the distance, Erik ties the hands of the time travelers behind their backs and prods them across the beach to sit with the band of captured monks.

While Erik warms his hands at a fire, Spencer whispers to Ethan, "The eye of Odin looks a lot like the beam from a laser pointer."

Ethan nods.

"Jake must be alive," Spencer says with relief. His smile fades. "Didn't I promise to eat his jacket if he found a way to use that laser pointer on this trip?"

Ethan nods again, grinning broadly.

"I hope he's got some mustard in one of those pockets," Spencer says dismally. "That jacket needs seasoning."

"Quiet!" Erik shouts from the fireside. "No talking, not if you want to keep your tongue!"

The minutes crawl by. Ethan wonders what Jake's plan might be.

Lure the Vikings away and sneak back to rescue his friends? That must be it, but what about their guard? Will Jake confront Erik or will he try to lure the boy away with another trick?

Ethan's thoughts are interrupted as a bright pink globe bounces and spins slowly along the beach. Ethan nudges Spencer and nods toward the tumbling shape.

"A balloon?" Spencer whispers.

"Or the world's biggest hunk of bubble gum," Ethan retorts.

"More tricks from Jake's utility vest," Spencer says with amazement. "I'll never make fun of his crazy comic-book ideas again."

The movement of the balloon catches Erik's attention. With gaping mouth, the yellow-haired Viking watches it roll toward him in the gusting breeze. As it draws near, Erik dives aside, dodging the strange object. Ethan and Spencer explode with laughter as the boy warrior shrinks from the harmless rubber globe.

The balloon bounces past the frightened Viking boy and picks up speed as the breeze grows stronger. Hearing the laughter, Erik's face reddens. He draws his sword and chases after the balloon, but the wind pushes the sphere further ahead.

Suddenly Jake crouches at Ethan's side.

"I meant for the balloon to distract him," Jake says. "Who knew he'd chase it?"

With his pocketknife, Jake saws the ropes binding his friends.

"It took you long enough to get here," Spencer complains. "How come you're not dead?"

Jake raps his knuckles against his stomach, a solid knocking sound. "The monk's package," he says, "I hid it inside my jacket. Spear-proof armor."

Spencer slaps his forehead.

"But there's blood," Spencer says, pointing to the torn fabric.

"The spear was already bloody," Jake explains. "Some of it rubbed off when that spear knocked the wind out of me."

"Where are the Vikings?" Ethan asks.

"I stayed out of sight and got them to chase the laser pointer beam halfway across the island," Jake says. "I taped it to a limb and left it shining into a sinkhole. The last I saw them, they were digging in that hole, looking for something."

"The treasure of Odin," Ethan laughs.

As they talk, Jake has freed one of the monks. He hands his knife to the monk. "Help the others get loose. Scatter across the island."

Spencer has a gleam in his eyes. "Why walk, when we can travel in style?" he asks. "If the monks will help, we can take one of those boats and make it to the mainland. Imagine the look in Forkbeard's beady eye when he sees that we've jacked one of his ships!"

"If we steal their boat, the Vikings will come after us for sure," Ethan says. "If we run away, they might decide we're not worth the trouble of chasing."

"Besides," adds Jake, "what do we know about boats?"

"I guess you're right," Spencer agrees, looking wistfully at the longboats drifting off-shore. "Let's get moving."

The monks scatter in groups of two or three. The time travelers jog along the waterline, planning to follow the shore to the causeway.

"If the tide's not too high," Ethan begins, but a shout cuts him off.

Erik reappears from his balloon chase. He's not alone. He holds a monk by the collar of his robe and presses the blade of his axe to the monk's throat.

"That guy sure chose the wrong direction," Spencer says.

"If you run," Erik shouts, "I'll make this monk a shorter man."

"I haven't been chased around so much since the day I visited the animal shelter with a hamburger in my pocket," Jake groans.

"Don't hurt him," Ethan calls. "We give up."

Erik pushes the ashen faced monk up the beach until he stands a few feet from the time travelers. With a sudden shift of his axe, Erik bangs the flat of the blade against his prisoner's skull. The monk's eyes roll back and he collapses in a tangle of black cloth.

"When he wakes up, his head will hurt," Erik gloats, "but at least he'll still have a head. You won't be so lucky."

Jake takes a step toward the Viking boy with the yellow braids dangling under his helmet.

"You're going to let us go," Jake assures him.

"Why would I do that?" Erik asks. He steps closer, standing nose to nose with Jake.

"You're the pipsqueak on this raid," Jake says, "the one they push around. Do you really think you're going to get a decent share of the plunder?"

"I'll get my share," Erik says defiantly.

"Only if you listen to me," Jake says.

Erik studies Jake curiously.

"Let us go without a fight," Jake continues, "and I'll put silver in your hands and precious stones. Hide the goodies. Keep it a secret. It will be all yours."

"You lie," Erik says.

Jake reaches into his jacket, and removes the bundle given by the dying monk. He loosens the leather, unwrapping a book bound in hammered silver with sparkling gems.

"Let me see that," Spencer says, snatching the book. Erik's greedy eyes follow the book as it changes hands.

"Maybe I'll take it away from you," Erik says.

"I'm as big as you are," Jake reminds him. "And there are three of us." Behind Erik, the unconscious monk moans and rubs his head. "Four as soon as he wakes up."

Spencer looks up from the book, his expression dazed. "No way we're giving this to Goldilocks," he says.

Jake shoots him an exasperated glare. "Don't go all Library-of-Congress on me, Spencer. I'm trying to keep the beach from getting bloody. It's just a book."

"But it's not," Spencer sputters. "This is *The Lindisfarne Gospels*. It belongs in a museum."

"Gospels?" Erik mocks. "Stories about the carpenter on a cross? You keep your holy book and give me the covers. Silver and jewels for me, words for you."

"What about it, Spencer?" Jake pleads.

Spencer swallows and says, "All right. Let me do it."

Prying his pocketknife between spine and covers, Spencer works the pages loose in a single clump. The gem-crusted cover falls to the rocky ground. At the clatter of falling metal, the monk groans again and sits up on the beach.

Thrusting the manuscript pages into the monk's hands, Spencer says, "Go! Hide! Keep this book safe."

When the monk hesitates, Spencer gives him a light push toward the inland.

"Do it for the monastery," Spencer urges him. "Do it for people a thousand years in the future."

Clutching the bundle of pages against his chest, the monk rises and stumbles from the shore. As the figure dwindles, Erik stuffs the jeweled book cover inside his wool shirt.

"On your way," Erik says. "I'm not an oath breaker, but if the others come back and find you here, I cannot help you."

Jake nods.

"Let's roll," he says to his friends.

As they move down the beach, Erik calls after them.

"If we meet again," the Viking says, "we meet as enemies."

Jake grins and calls back, "Anytime, anywhere, Erik. I'm ready whenever you are."

"Give it a rest!" Spencer says. "Can you tone down the macho? You sound like you're auditioning for a kung fu flick."

Jake ignores Spencer and mumbles, "He can't be that tough. He wears pigtails."

The friends from the future follow the shoreline toward the causeway. Despite the rising tide, they hope to cross the land bridge. As they detour around an inlet, Spencer points out three monks at the water's edge.

"They have a boat," Spencer says.

"Maybe we can get a ride," Jake suggests.

The monks are heaving the boat into the sea as the boys approach. A freckled monk with a wispy brown beard recognizes Jake.

"You freed us from the Northmen," he says, gripping Jake's hand. "Come with us. The raiders won't chase us into the mainland woods."

Together the six of them launch the boat, wetting their clothes to the waist. Spencer finds a dry blanket and wraps it around himself. No wind fills the sail, so two monks work the oars while Freckle-face watches for floating debris in the foggy sea. Ethan settles beside him and asks, "Have you seen a visitor to the island, a tall man with red hair, a mark like a half-moon on his cheek?"

"I haven't," the thin-bearded man answers. "We are a small community. If such a man came to Holy Isle, I would have met him."

Ethan nods, trying to hide his disappointment.

After a moment, Freckle-face adds, "The Good Shepherd will help you find your lost sheep."

"Thanks," Ethan says sincerely. "I've just started looking, and I won't give up."

They pass the rest of the short voyage in silence except for the splashing of the oars. As the boat grinds onto the beach of the mainland, the passengers scramble onto the pebbled shore, again wetting their clothes.

"Will you stay with us?" the freckled monk asks.

"We have our own way home," Ethan replies. "Thanks for the ride."

"The Northmen will be gone soon," Brother Freckles assures them.

"But they'll come back," Spencer warns. "And they'll keep coming."

"Then pray for us," the monk says.

"I will," Spencer promises.

As the monks drag their boat above the tide line, the time travelers follow the shore north.

"How are we going to pray for people that have been dead a thousand years?" Jake asks.

"God is bigger than time," Ethan says.

 **TURN TO PAGE 188.**

GOD'S CLOCK

Is God really bigger than time?

To find out what the Bible says about God and time, use the message wheel below. Start with the circled letter on top, then move to the right reading every other letter. So the first letter is w, the second letter is i, and the third letter is t. When you've gone around the wheel twice, you'll have the whole message figured out.

ANSWER: With the Lord a day is like a thousand years and a thousand years are like a day (2 Peter 3:9)

Ethan loves Spencer like a brother, but what is the best way to show that love? He leans close to his bookworm buddy.

"You need time to get your asthma under control," he breathes into Spencer's ear. "Who's the best dodge-ball player you ever saw?"

Spencer points a finger at Ethan's chest. Ethan nods.

"Let's see if I'm as good at dodge-spear," Ethan says.

Spencer shakes his head, panic in his eyes. Ethan squeezes his shoulder and grins.

"I have a surprise for the Vikings, something their shields won't stop and their swords won't slice," Ethan says, sounding more confident than he feels. "Do you remember the nut trees Brother Kelvyn showed us?"

Spencer nods.

157

"Meet me there," Ethan whispers.

Spencer grabs at Ethan's sleeve, but the bigger boy pulls free. He slithers through the bushes and crawls along the ground. As he wriggles through the bushes, a fallen tree branch blocks his way, a straight stick about six feet long. Ethan rises slowly to a crouch and picks up the stick.

"Not much of a weapon," he murmurs, "but better than nothing."

Bending low, Ethan puts another twenty yards between himself and Spencer's hiding place.

Leaping out of the brush, Ethan shouts, "Free gold!" He waves the stick in the air. "Come and get it! "

Ethan sprints east through the fog. If he falls or turns an ankle, it's all over. His pursuers will be on him in seconds.

Ethan glances back. The Vikings are closer. The younger raider, the one named Erik, leads his partner by several yards. With his war axe lifted high, the Viking boy draws nearer with each second. If Ethan doesn't reach his destination soon…

Something buzzes his ear. Seconds later, a tiny form veers past his face.

Ethan glances toward the gray sky and pants, "Thank you."

Squat shapes appear on the ground around him. Emerging from the fog are a dozen knee-high boxes built from slabs of wet, glistening slate. A faint humming fills the air. Back home, this sound

would be a warning, but now the low drone is sweet music.

Without slowing, Ethan swings the long stick at one of the slate boxes. The slabs of stone scatter apart and a swarm of enraged bees swirls into the air behind him. The wooden stick topples another hive, and more bees explode from their home. Running fast, the Viking boy Erik cannot turn in time. He bursts into the thick cloud of furious insects. He bats and swats at the stinging honeybees.

Ethan continues to run, distancing himself from the field of beehives. The monks keep the bees both for honey and for beeswax from which they make candles.

The spear-toting Viking, the one who stabbed Jake, turns like a frightened rabbit. Waving both arms about his head, he runs away yelping and whimpering with every sting.

The yellow-haired Norwegian boy stumbles away from the honey yard, and the circling bees trickle back to their ruined hives. The boy's face is puffy, one eye swollen shut. He weaves, staggers, and thumps to the ground like a bag of potatoes.

Ethan doesn't like these Vikings, and he hates what they are doing to the monks, but he can't ignore this hurting boy. This many bee stings can kill. Maybe he can help.

A voice calls Ethan's name and he spins around to see Spencer approaching, making a wide detour around the honey yard.

"How's the asthma?" Ethan asks.

Spencer holds an inhaler in his hand.

"I got better as soon as I could use this," he says. "Thanks for playing tag with those killers."

"Next time, you're It," Ethan tells him.

The time travelers kneel on either side of the yellow-haired boy. Erik moans and glares at them with his good eye.

"We'll do what we can," Ethan promises. "Keep still."

"Let's get those stingers out of his skin," Spencer says, "but don't pull them out with your fingers."

"Why?"

"Each stinger has a venom sack," Spencer explains. "If you pinch the stinger between your fingers, it pumps the rest of the poison into his body."

"Like squeezing a tube of toothpaste?" Ethan asks. "I didn't know that."

Spencer pulls a pocketknife from his jeans. He opens the blade and uses the edge to cautiously drag a stinger from the Viking's cheek. With his own folding knife, Ethan follows Spencer's lead. The Viking boy's long-sleeved shirt and pants of heavy leather protected his body while the iron helmet shielded his head. Most of the stingers are buried in his neck, face, and hands. The friends work quickly, but carefully. Soon all the stingers have been scraped from his flesh. Erik groans and slips into unconsciousness.

"Will he be okay?" Ethan wonders.

"I hope so." Spencer shrugs. "There's nothing more we can do for him."

"Maybe there's one more thing," Ethan says. He bows his head and prays, "God, watch over this boy and show him your love."

"Amen," Spencer says.

"Now we've got to meet Jake at the nut grove," Ethan says.

Spencer grabs his arm. "Jake took a spear in the gut," he says. "He's not going to meet us anywhere."

"I'll explain on the way," Ethan tells his friend, leading him into the mist. "How do you think Jake got rid of the monk's bundle? He must have hidden it inside his coat. The spear stabbed the package, not Jake."

"But we saw blood on his coat," Spencer protests.

"There was already blood on the spear head," Ethan reminds him. "The spear slammed Jake down and knocked the breath out of him. We led the Vikings away so he'd have time to recover."

"We were decoys?"

"Right," Ethan agrees. "When Jake said he'd see us in history, what do you think he meant? What's the only class all three of us share?"

"History class," Spencer says, his face brightening, "taught by Mr. Nutt! So we're heading for the nut trees to meet Jake."

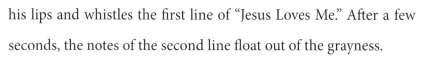

Ahead of them, tall shapes loom in the fog. Ethan whispers, "We're there, but how do we find Jake without bringing the Vikings down on us?"

"Leave it to me." Spencer puckers his lips and whistles the first line of "Jesus Loves Me." After a few seconds, the notes of the second line float out of the grayness.

"It's us," Ethan calls softly. "Are you all right?"

Jake comes out of the mist, smiling. He makes a mock salute. "Ready for action."

The athlete opens his torn coat and reveals the leather package stuffed under his belt.

"Let's scope out the thing that saved my life," he says.

 TURN TO **PAGE 164**.

Jake unwraps the layers of leather and drops them to the grass. Inside the wrapping he finds a book about fourteen inches high and ten inches wide. Precious stones glitter in the silver-plated cover. The spear point pierced the layers of leather and stabbed the cover, but the pages are undamaged.

"Know anything about this?" Jake asks, offering the book to Spencer.

Spencer leafs through the pages. He stares at a page filled with strange birds and fish, surrounded in interlocking lines of bright color. His hands tremble.

"Incredible!" Spencer says in a choked voice. "This is *The Lindisfarne Gospels.* All four gospels, hand-written in Latin and decorated with amazing art. It's in the British Museum—or it will be in 1,200 years."

"He's going to cry," Jake jokes to Ethan.

"I might," Spencer says. He lays the book gently on the leather wrappings and launches himself at Jake. Wrapping the bigger boy in a bear hug, he says, "You and your stupid pocket coat saved one the world's most precious books."

"Awesome," Jake says, untangling from the hug. "I'll give you my autograph when we get home. But what do we do with it?"

"Since we can't take it back with us…" Spencer breaks off and looks at Ethan with pleading in his eyes. "We can't, can we?"

"Nope," Ethan says. "The machine won't bring anything from the past."

Spencer sighs heart-brokenly. "So we either hide this or find someone who will protect it."

IF YOU THINK THE TIME CRASHERS SHOULD HIDE THE BOOK, TURN TO **PAGE 166**.

IF YOU THINK THE BOYS SHOULD FIND SOMEONE TO KEEP THE BOOK, TURN TO **PAGE 169**.

W e'd better hide it," Ethan decides. "The longer we carry the book around, the more likely some Viking robs us."

Using their pocket knives, the boys cut and lift a piece of sod. They gouge out the soft soil underneath to make a hole. Rewrapping the book in the waterproof leather, Spencer settles it in the hole as if he were putting a baby to bed. They throw away the excess dirt and press the sod back in place. They lay small stones on the sod in the shape of a cross.

"I hope that catches the attention of the monks," Spencer says.

"We need to spy on the raiders," Ethan tells his friends. "If my dad's on this island, the Vikings might have captured him."

As the three friends hike toward the sea, the earth suddenly falls away sharply in a steep, muddy slope.

"No zip line," Jake says, grinning, "so I guess we slide."

Easing over the edge of the drop, the athlete rides the slope on his backside.

"Yahoo!" Spencer yelps, pushing off from the edge with Ethan behind him. They land in a tumble at the bottom, but their laughter dies, smothered by the thuds of heavy boots.

"Good news," Jake says. "Looks like we won't have to find the Vikings."

Six bearlike warriors close in on the boys. Seizing their arms with bruising strength, the Vikings march the three friends through the fog. They pass the bloody body of a black-robed monk beside the path. In a few minutes they arrive at the invaders'  camp beside the water. On the beach, the Vikings warm their hands by driftwood bonfires. A goat on a spit sizzles and browns over one of the fires. Isolated on the edge of the camp, twenty or thirty monks sit on the wet rocks, lashed together with strong ropes. Most are bloodied and bruised. The three dragon ships bob just off shore, rising and falling on the gentle waves. The captors push the three boys toward the monks and shove them onto the ground.

"Don't make us tie you," grunts one of the Vikings, a man with a white scar crossing his forehead. "I'm hungry enough to eat a whole goat, but I'll be watching you. If I have to interrupt my supper to chase you down, I'll be very angry." He leans close to Jake and adds, "You won't like me when I'm angry."

"I already don't like you," Jake says.

The Viking roars with laughter and punches Jake on the shoulder.

"Behave and I'll bring you leftovers," the scarred man promises.

 TURN TO **PAGE 90**.

’d feel better if we could put this in someone's hands," Spencer says.

Ethan points through the shifting fog. "Is that a house?"

Through the mist, they see a hut made of woven sticks and mud plaster. Before they can approach, a voice booms through the mist.

"Friends, be welcome in the home of Marcas the smith; enemies, be wary," says a bull-necked man holding a heavy hammer. A leather shirt strains to cover his broad chest and muscular arms. "Which are you?"

"We're not enemies," Ethan says. "Not Vikings."

"Vikings?" growls the man named Marcas. He tightens his grip on the heavy iron hammer. "Is that the noise and flame from the monastery? The Northmen?"

"It's terrible," Spencer says. "The Vikings are killing the monks, stealing and burning."

A woman hobbles from the hut, leaning on a crutch. She is slender, her pretty face marked by strong cheekbones and bright eyes. A dingy bandage wraps one foot. She lays a hand on the blacksmith's burly arm. "Go, husband. The monks need you."

His gruff expression softens as he turns to her. "And leave you alone, Emer, with an injured foot?"

"I can fend for myself," she says fiercely.

"I know, wife," he says. "That's why I'm staying, to protect any foolish Vikings that might cross your path."

Marcas turns his gaze back to the three boys. He runs a hand through thinning brown hair. "You have the look of outlanders. Do you have a place to hide from the raiders?"

"We're not looking for shelter," Ethan tells the thickset man. "We have something that must be guarded from the Vikings."

Jake steps forward and holds out the jeweled book. Marcas strokes the silver-plated cover with soot-blackened fingers.

"A monk died to save this book," Jake tells him. "Can you keep it safe?"

The blacksmith nods solemnly. He hands the book to his wife Emer.

"I am a peaceful man," Marcas says, "but I will safeguard this

Bible. If more blood is spilled over this book, it will be Viking blood."

Watching the blacksmith's fingers whiten on the grip of the hammer, Ethan is glad to have him as a friend instead of an enemy. Emer opens the curtain that hangs in the doorway of their home and invites the boys inside.

"Thanks, but we're looking for a man with red hair and a birthmark on his cheek," Ethan says. "Have you seen him?"

Marcas and Emer shake their heads.

"We have to keep looking," Ethan tells them.

"The book is safe with me," Marcas says.

"We pray for your good hunting," Emer adds.

Before he turns away, Ethan says to Marcas, "There are a lot of Vikings. What if a whole gang comes here to your house?"

Marcas smiles. Something dangerous flickers in his eyes.

"I'll get a bigger hammer," he says.

Waving goodbye to the blacksmith and his wife, the three friends set off into the gray day. The mist quickly swallows the hut.

"Do you think *The Lindisfarne Gospels* will be safe with Marcas?" Spencer wonders.

Jake laughs. "Would you want to tangle with that guy? Pity the Viking who lays his greedy hands on that book."

They walk in silence for a few minutes until Spencer says, "I don't think your dad has been here, Ethan."

"I'm thinking the same thing," Ethan says dejectedly. "It's a small island. If a man appeared in futuristic clothes with a moon-shaped birthmark on his face, somebody would remember him."

"Maybe we should head to the mainland," Jake says. "We can look for your dad over there, and we'll be close to the removal bus—"

"Retrieval pulse," Spencer corrects him.

"We'll be close to the removal bus in case we need to leave in a hurry," Jake finishes.

"Okay," Ethan agrees. "That makes sense."

"We'd better hurry," Spencer warns. "The tide is rising. Pretty soon we'll be trapped here on the island."

Even in the fog, Ethan's sense of direction guides them to the land bridge.

"Whoa!" Ethan says. "You're right about the tide, Spencer."

"He's always right," Jake groans. "Right is his middle name."

The walkway is skinnier than before. In places the gray water washes back and forth over the causeway.

"Can we make it?" Jake asks.

Spencer chews his lower lip as he studies the heaving waves. "I think so," he says. "I hope we don't have to swim in that freezing water."

The boys set off jogging along the causeway, clumping through mud and splashing in shallow water. Their feet feel like lumps of ice. The pools of water grow wider and deeper, sometimes rising over their ankles.

"We're over halfway," Spencer says. "We're going to make it. No prob—"

A low growling cuts off Spencer's words. Glaring eyes pierce the mist before them. A dozen dog-like shapes appear, but bigger and shaggier than any dog they've ever seen.

"Wolves," Spencer whispers, splashing to a sudden stop. "Maybe I was wrong about no problems."

"Now you decide to be wrong?" Jake moans. "In the middle of the ocean with a pack of wolves? Great timing, Brainiac."

"Don't panic," Spencer says. "I've read that wolves rarely attack people."

The wolf pack slouches forward, heads low and fur bristling. The lead wolf growls and creeps closer to the time travelers.

"Yeah, but have they read that book?" Jake asks.

Ethan wonders why the wolf pack is heading to the island. Can they smell the blood from the Viking violence? If so, the wolves are hungry and agitated. Maybe the noise and smoke have angered them. He pulls up a Bible verse on his tablet, but the letters are hopelessly jumbled. He shoves the device back into his pocket.

"Do we turn back or try to swim around them?" Ethan asks.

 TURN TO **PAGE 178**.

LEFT, RIGHT, OR WRONG?

Ethan's tablet is really messed up. This is a tough one! You'll need a telephone to figure it out. On your phone each number has some letters with it. For instance, in this message, 3 is either D or E or F. You have to decide which letter goes with each number.

3-6   6-6-8   8-8-7-6   8-6   8-4-3   7-4-4-4-8   6-7   8-4-3
5-3-3-8;   5-3-3-7   9-6-8-7   3-6-6-8   3-7-6-6   3-8-4-5.

Let's take our chances with the fur-balls," Spencer says.

"What could go wrong?" Jake asks. "They only outnumber us four to one."

"I'm good with animals," Spencer assures them.

Moving step by careful step, the brainy time traveler approaches the wolves. The pack leader crouches, primed to pounce. His threatening growl grows louder.

"Good doggy," Spencer says in a gentle voice. He shuffles forward. "If I had a ball, we'd have some fun, wouldn't we? You're just a big puppy."

The lead wolf curls his lips and bares yellow fangs.

"Grandma, what big teeth you have," Spencer says cheerfully. "But you don't want to eat me. These other guys are bigger and plumper. I'd barely be an appetizer."

Still pacing forward, talking softly, Spencer draws near enough to pet the wolf's shaggy head. Taking baby steps, the young genius

pushes on, moving an inch at a time in the rising water. The growling beast takes a step back. Dropping his tail, he slinks to one side. The other wolves follow suit, the pack parting in the middle.

"Easy does it," Spencer instructs his friends. "Don't hurry. And don't be afraid. They can smell fear."

"Oh, man," Jake says. "I hope my deodorant doesn't dry up."

Seconds crawl as the boys pass through the pack. As they clear the last wolf, the boys turn, walking backwards, keeping the pack in sight. The wolves turn away and trot toward the island, silent except for the splashing of their paws.

"That was a close one," Spencer gasps, wiping cold sweat from his face.

"Give that boy an A+ for dog training!" Jake offers a high five and Spencer weakly slaps his hand.

"Don't thank me," Spencer says. "God's watching over us."

"Sure," Ethan agrees. "If God can part the Red Sea for Moses and his buddies, parting the gray wolves is a piece of cake."

"Unless we're counting on God to part this gray water for us, we'd better make tracks," Jake suggests.

"Or make splashes," Ethan calls as they trot through the rising tide.

By the time their feet crunch on the rocky beach, the boys are soaked. Laughing with relief, they flop on the damp ground.

"We are unbeatable," Spencer says, pumping one fist in the moist air.

"We beat the wolves," Jake agrees.

"We beat the water," Ethan echoes.

"But can you beat Wiglaf the warrior?" demands a harsh voice.

A Viking stands over them, glaring. He holds a double-edged sword and a battle-axe.

"A guard," Ethan grumbles.

"And he's built like a lineman for the NFL," Jake says. "Still, there are three of us and one of him."

"Count again, boy," Wiglaf says with a crooked grin, his face framed with greasy blond hair. "Wiglaf is one. My sword, Iron-Tooth, is two. And my axe, Shield-Biter, is three."

"That's pretty good math," Spencer admits.

"What will you do with us?" Ethan asks.

"If you behave like good little lambs," Wiglaf explains, "we'll wait for the tide to leave, and I'll take you to our jarl Ivar Forkbeard. He'll sell you as slaves."

"And if we don't behave?" Ethan asks.

"Then you'll meet my friends," Wiglaf says, shaking the sword and axe at the boys.

Ethan searches his brain for a way out. Chopped into fish

bait or carried off in slavery. If they could get in position for the retrieval pulse...

"What do you say?" Wiglaf asks. He nudges Ethan with his soft leather boot. "The easy way or the dead way?"

"We promise not to fight or run if you do us one favor," Ethan says.

Wiglaf eyes Ethan skeptically and runs thick fingers through his beard.

"No favors," he says.

"We are followers of Jesus," Ethan hurries on. He jerks his head in the direction of the great stone cross barely visible through the clouds of fog. "Let us worship at his cross and we'll give you no trouble."

 TURN TO **PAGE 185**.

WRITTEN IN STONE

The tall stone crosses created by the Irish and Scottish monks were like books carved in stone, covered with art that reminded people of Bible stories. Try drawing scenes from some of your favorite Bible stories inside the cross on page 184. After you finish drawing, you can also color your drawings.

If you have trouble remembering stories from the Bible, here are some to help you get started.

Jesus is born in a stable (Luke 2:4-7)

Jesus brings a dead girl back to life (Mark 5:35-43)

Jesus blesses little children (Mark 10:13-16)

Jesus heals people (Mark 10:46-52)

Jesus feeds hungry people (Mark 6:30-44)

Jesus walks on water (Mark 6:45-52)

Jesus dies on the cross (Mark 15:25-37)

Jesus rises from the dead (Matthew 28:1-10)

Why not worship a real god like Thor the thunderer or All-Father Odin?" Wiglaf throws back his shaggy head and laughs. "Can a carpenter on a cross save you?"

"Take us to the cross, and we'll show you what Jesus can do," Ethan promises.

"No favors!" Wiglaf roars again. He cocks his head at the boys, then glances toward the stone cross. "But you've given me an idea. I'm in the mood for a nap, and I can't risk you cutting my throat while I sleep."

He kicks Ethan.

"Up, all three of you," he grunts. He lays the point of Iron-Tooth between Ethan's shoulder blades. "If anyone tries to run, this one dies."

He herds the friends to the high cross and makes them sit at its base, their backs against the carved stone. From a bag at his belt, the Viking brings out a length of rope. He loops it around each boy's neck once, wraps it snugly around the stone cross and knots it with a sailor's skill.

"Sit still and you'll keep your breath," Wiglaf advises them. "Struggle and you'll strangle." The Viking chuckles as he stretches out on the ground and pulls a blanket over his legs. "Struggle and strangle! That's good."

"He has a sense of humor," Spencer observes. "I guess he's not all bad."

"At least he enjoys his work," Jake agrees.

Ethan takes a deep breath in relief. He and his friends are back at the cross where they first arrived. As the tide laps the shore, Ethan feels a familiar sensation, a tingle in his spine and pinpricks on his skin. The retrieval pulse! The three boys exchange knowing looks.

"Everybody on board the removal bus," Jake whispers.

"*Retrieval pulse!*" Spencer chides.

"Hey, Wiglaf," Ethan calls. "Are you sure the Carpenter can't save us?"

"Hush, boy," Wiglaf snorts. "I'm trying to sleep."

"You don't want to sleep through this!" Ethan insists. "I'm praying for Jesus to take us home. Why don't you pray to Thor to keep us here? We'll see which is the real God."

"Enough noise!" Kicking off the blanket, the Viking springs to his feet. He stalks toward Ethan with the axe Shield-Biter in his meaty fist. "I warned you."

Hair springs up on the nape of Ethan's neck. Electricity dances on his hands and face. His guts feel as if they are turning upside down as the retrieval pulse strengthens. The angry Wiglaf looms over him, axe lifted.

"Think about it, Wiglaf," Ethan says as the world blurs. "Thor or Jesus? Are you sure?"

A heart-beat later, the boys disappear, leaving limp ropes on the shore and a bewildered Viking staring at the high cross.

THE END

 SEE EPILOGUE, PAGE 194.

Was that boat cool or what?" Spencer says, still wrapped in the coarse, wool blanket. "It's called a currach, a wooden frame with a leather covering. They soak the leather in wool grease to make it waterproof."

"A leather boat?" Jake asks. "That doesn't sound safe."

"Currachs are very sturdy. An Irish monk named Brendan sailed a leather boat all the way from Ireland to North America," Spencer explains. "He got there a thousand years before Columbus."

Jake throws up his hands in amazement. "How do you cram so much junk into your head?"

"I buy big hats," Spencer says, grinning.

The three boys round a bend in the shore and the outline of the high cross appears in the fog. At the same moment, a light wind parts the mist revealing a bear-like Viking standing near the cross. Pointing a sword toward the Time Crashers, the Viking grunts, "Who's there?"

"I'll handle him," says Jake.

Ethan nods to his athletic friend. "Okay, game on."

Jake mock salutes his buddies, then strides toward the Viking.

"You must have lost the thumb wrestling match," Jake says. "Your pals are grabbing all the loot while you rot on guard duty."

"Surrender," the Viking commands, "or face the sword of Wiglaf."

Jake continues to amble toward the guard. "Wiglaf? Is that really your name? I'll bet the kids gave you a hard time in kindergarten."

From one of the pockets on his vest, Jake takes out a red tube about nine inches long.

"I've brought you a present, Wiggy," Jake says.

Wiglaf grins crookedly and lifts his sword. "Come on, then. Your red stick against my sword Iron-Tooth. Your mother will soon gather wood for your funeral fire."

"Fire?" Jake asks. "Funny that you'd bring that up."

The athlete extends the red tube toward Wiglaf and twists a cap from one end. The Viking watches curiously. Jake brings the outside of the cap near the tip of the tube. Just before he knocks them together, Jake closes his eyes and promises, "Wiggy, this is gonna light up your life."

The road flare erupts in blinding flame, the tip blazing. Wiglaf yelps like a cat caught in a sprinkler. Stumbling backwards, he drops Iron-Tooth and raises an arm to shield his eyes. In the same heartbeat, Jake flings the flaming flare to the ground and launches himself at the Viking in a perfect tackle. The raider hits the beach with a loud "Whoof!" As Jake straddles the Viking's waist, Wiglaf struggles for the battle-axe hung at his belt. With an unexpected lurch, the warrior rolls over, pinning Jake to the rocky ground. Wiglaf lifts the axe for a killing blow, but freezes when he feels the point of his own sword pressed against the nape of his neck. Ethan stands over him, the weapon held in steady hands.

"Throw away the axe," Ethan advises, "and maybe Iron-Tooth won't bite."

The Viking obeys and Jake scrambles free. Still holding the sword pointed at Wiglaf, Ethan orders, "Make yourself useful. Gather some sticks for a fire."

As the Viking turns away, grumbling under his breath, Ethan winks at his friends and whispers, "That should keep him busy for a few minutes."

Pinpricks tingle the skin of the time travelers. A faint hum buzzes in the air.

"Now would be a good time to apologize for making fun of my utility vest," Jake says, smiling smugly. "You have to admit, the flare

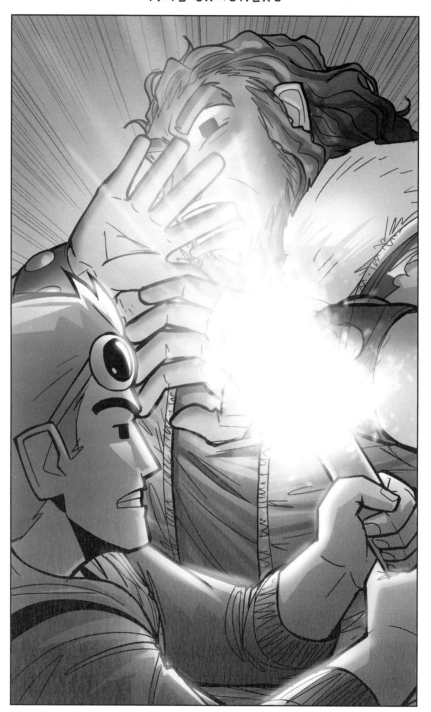

saved our bacon."

"Hey, I'm your biggest fan," Spencer insists. "I want you to expand your operation. Get a Jake signal to shine on the clouds at night. Maybe a Jake cave where you can park the Jake-mobile."

Jake pounds his fist into an open palm. "One of these days, Brain Boy, I'm going to send you to the moon."

"Cool," Spencer says. "Can we fly there in the Jake plane?"

"I'm warning—"

The argument falls silent, as if cut off by a slamming door. Wiglaf peers around the empty beach in confusion. The three strangers are nowhere to be seen.

THE END

Epilogue

We're back," Ethan says. "Is everybody okay?"

His friends nod, the ruby glow of the power crystal tinting their faces.

"What a trip," Spencer says. "When do we go again?"

"Soon," Ethan promises. He wonders where and when the time machine will send them on the next trip as he continues to search for his father. Who knew history could be so fascinating—and so dangerous?

Jake glances at the time machine's digital clock.

"We're in time for the game," Jake tells his friends.

"Once a jock," Spencer moans, "always a jock."

TIME CRASHERS

"My house in an hour," Jake insists. "Pizza. HD TV. Gridiron action!"

"Who's playing?" Ethan asks.

"Are you sure you want to know?" Jake asks.

"Yeah, who's playing?" Ethan repeats.

Jake grins mischievously. "The Vikings and the Saints."

The Real Deal

Did the things in this story really happen? Some of them.

Irish monks really did carry Christianity to many places, including Scotland and northern England. Lindisfarne was an important center of Christianity for centuries. Although the monastery is gone, tourists still enjoy visiting the island of Lindisfarne. But keep an eye on the tides. People who aren't careful might have to spend the night on the island.

There isn't really a standing cross at the causeway that leads to Holy Isle, but many of the tall stone crosses created by the Celtic monks still stand, scattered mostly throughout Ireland, Scotland, and Wales. The old crosses seem like time travelers from long ago.

The Lindisfarne Gospels truly is one of the world's most beautiful books. At one point the book was stolen by Vikings, but the monks later found it stripped of its jeweled cover. Today *The Lindisfarne Gospels* belong to the British Library. If you can't get to London, you can find pictures of the amazing pages on the Internet.

The Vikings did attack Lindisfarne on June 8, 793, probably the first Viking attack in England. They could be blood-thirsty raiders, but they also appreciated poetry, story-telling, music, trading, and family life. In their longboats, Viking explorers visited North America long before Columbus. The Vikings named North America Vinland because of the wild grapevines they saw there. They also sailed to Russia, Istanbul, and Baghdad.

Christian monasteries were favorite targets of the Viking raiders, and many Christian monks were captured or killed by the raiders. As the Vikings settled in Christian countries, they became Christians themselves. Christian missionaries also carried the message of Jesus to the Scandinavian homelands of the Vikings. In the end, the cross of Jesus was more powerful than the Viking sword.

TIME CRASHERS

What about Ethan, Jake, Spencer, and the Time Machine? Are they real? I'm not allowed to answer that, so don't ask. Really, just don't ask because I can't talk about it. All I can tell you is that the adventure has barely begun. The Viking raid was a vacation for the boys compared to what's coming next: major danger, massive destruction, and more weird things from Jake's pockets.

DON'T MISS THE NEXT TIME CRASHERS TRIP!